The Two Moons of Mars

A Pilgrimage of Southern Ancestry and Faith

KENNETH HALL

Doghouse
Dreams LLC

COPYRIGHT

Author: Kenneth Hall, kennyrhall@yahoo.com
Editor: Brian Darnell, bkdarnell@comcast.net
Artist: Amber Leigh, DoghouseDreams@gmail.com

Copyright © 2015 by Kenneth R. Hall   Publisher: Doghouse Dreams LLC

U.S. Copyright Case #1-3148941271 • ISBN 978-0-9966308-0-1

Doghouse Dreams LLC   2810 Southfield Trail
Cumming, Georgia 30040
www.doghousedreams.com

Ordering Information
. Available at Amazon.com, Amazon Europe, and www.TwoMoonsofMars.com.
. E-book can be purchased and downloaded for Kindle.
. Author signed copies can be purchased direct from Publisher at
  www.DoghouseDreams.com or TwoMoonsofMars.com
. Watch for upcoming Audiobook at Audible.com.

Printed in the United States of America by CreateSpace, an Amazon company.

Unless otherwise noted, all photographs taken by the author. Ruskin Cave Colony photograph retrieved from yesteryearsnews.wordpress.com. Life Magazine photo from historical sources. George Chevrie photo from Randolph County Heritage Museum. Ruth Asawa photo from www.sfsota.org.

For Pam...and the Highway

TABLE OF CONTENTS

TABLE OF CONTENTS (cont'd)

« FOREWARD »

Around 1720, Jonathan Swift began writing *Travels into Several Remote Nations of the World in Four Parts*, by Lemuel Gulliver, later published as *Gulliver's Travels*. Five years later, he finished his work, and its first publishing in 1726 was met with such popularity that the book sold ten thousand copies in its first three weeks. In the novel, Swift's main character, Gulliver, comments on several discoveries of the astronomers on the flying island of Laputa, including their description of the moons of Mars:

"...two lesser stars, or satellites, which revolve around Mars, whereof the innermost is distant from the center of the primary exactly three of his diameters, and the outermost five: the former revolves in the space of ten hours, and the latter in twenty-one and a half."

In August of 1877, working with the world's largest telescope at the time, located at the U. S. Naval Observatory in Washington, D.C., professor and astronomer Asaph Hall discovered the two moons of Mars. Based upon the gods of Fear and Dread in Book XV of the Iliad, he named them "Phobos" and "Deimos." Hall later determined that the larger moon, Phobos, completed a rotation around Mars in 7.7 hours, while Deimos completed its orbit in 30.3 hours. Swift's estimates of 10 hours for Phobos and 21.5 hours for Deimos were off target by only 2.3 hours and 8.8 hours, respectively. His predictive accuracy of the two moons of Mars predated their actual discovery by one hundred and fifty-two years and remains one of the great literary mysteries of all time.

« EDITOR'S PREFACE »
By Brian Darnell

In the fall of 2014, the author of *The Two Moons of Mars* sent me a manuscript of a story he had written for his children. "I want to leave something permanent behind," he told me. At first glance, what I discovered in the pages of the work we call "Moons" was a story not unlike other stories by other writers. As I read and re-read the story, eventually agreeing to serve as editor, collaborator, and often as creative jester and literary provocateur, I unearthed buried gems of philosophical truths, Southern wit and charm, and strands of faith that enticed me to join the author along his pilgrimage. With the turning of every page, the abstract pilgrimage transformed into a shared intimate journey, where I could see a revelation in his perspective, not unlike a lighthouse beacon in the distance which serves its purpose to warn by capturing one's attention.

I began to understand the parallels of a very personal journey that most are unwilling to confront, to discuss, or to bear out on the pages of a book; however, it was here on these pages that I heard the voice of a writer that welcomed me into a journey often wrought with treacherous rites of passage, universal truths, and renewed "nothing new under the sun" perspective on the everyday choices and circumstances that confront every generation, especially fathers and sons. There I discovered the orbital plane of my own humanity. There I learned that the journey is never one's own. Someone somewhere has taken that same step, felt that same strain of emotion, and been equally perplexed by the painfully complex simplicity of living life and being related to anyone by blood or bond. There I discovered that one person's story really is every person's story. We simply find a new story to tell, as one uncertain path begins where another ends.

What matters is how we live with or without choices and consequences and how we interact with others along the way. It is a path of steps and seconds that leads toward a terminal end which turns into a new beginning that is never, and was never, really new at all. Someone has been this way before, and someone will be back this way again, sooner or later. Happy orbiting!

Greers Ferry Lake from Jamestown Mountain, Batesville, Arkansas

« INTRODUCTION »

As I began the research for this book, I discovered connections between seemingly diverse individuals, places, and events across the generations. First published in 1908, the historical book, *Pioneers and Makers of Arkansas*, refers to my family: *"Away up on Poke Bayou, near where Batesville now stands, there came in 1814 a band of Peels and Millers from Kentucky"*. Over the next two hundred years, that "band of Peels" migrated south and west to Texas, moved up into the Missouri hill country, and even drifted back east to Tennessee. A few went north into Illinois and Michigan looking for work and liked it enough to stay. Others continued to settle and spread among the balds and narrows of the Ozarks and the thick forests of the Ouachita rise. Our genetic marker, our code, has been carried along in the same blood of misdirection as our pioneer ancestors, and continues to define the abilities and shortcomings and hopes and dreams of generations today, yielding similar successes and failures that guide and encourage, or bind and restrain, the opportunities presented and decisions made. Needing to understand better who I was, who I am, and who I could become, I found shadows of those answers through the illumination of the lives and events that blazed paths before me. Much contained herein is about my family, but it could really be a story about anyone's family, especially if you are a product of the South. I felt uprooted throughout most of my life, but as constant as the two moons of Mars are in their orbits, I discovered that there was always a connecting strand that held me to my past and gave me a place to be from and a place to long to return to.

Kenneth Hall

« PROLOGUE »

Kurt's gotta know. I have to tell him and get this off my chest. Will he understand? Will he be able to help me understand? I don't know but I have to tell him. How?

There was always a kinship that I felt with Levon Helm, a man I never met, but a bond existed between us, an intimacy of shared experience. It came through in his unique voice, that raspy southern drawl which spoke to me in the deep recesses of my soul and warmed my heart on the loneliest of difficult days. His voice always brought me home. Helm's personal story had the markings of a man well acquainted with adversity and sorrow, so the words of his songs always carried the weight of faithfulness and authenticity. Like me, he grew up in the Arkansas dirt, and could not wash it off no matter the length and breadth of his travels.

Music was also my compulsion. It was a great primordial force that lifted me like a child in its father's arms away from the cares of an overly complicated and too often brutal world. It moved me to tears, changed my perspective, flooded me with joy, prompted me to reminisce, and soothed my soul. A dreary morning not so long ago may have been the loneliest time of my life. The earth tilted on its axis and I tumbled into chaotic darkness which exited into a new and uncertain reality, and it happened faster and with more cruelty than imaginable. It was something akin to a new birth, spit out into a world so different than the one I was in before, unrecognizable, bewildered, and lost. Weeks passed in a monotonous routine of mindless existence, then months, and suddenly almost unconsciously, as if swimming frantically from beneath the water toward a pocket of trapped air, I picked up my cell phone and called my friend, Kurt. On the drive to Loveless Café outside of Nashville to meet him for breakfast, the sound of the soul of good company poured forth from my truck speakers, as my old friend Levon, a recent cancer survivor, sang his heart out on his inspired CD, *Dirt Farmer*.

Before the front door closed behind me, I smelled the biscuits, mingled among whiffs of coffee and open jars of sweet fruit jam and honey. The wooden slat floor creaked beneath my feet as the waitress led me to a table with a west facing window, from where I could see through the open blinds the exit ramp of the Natchez Trace northern terminus. Loveless was busy but less crowded this morning than many other visits. Sipping my freshly poured coffee, I pondered Helm's version of Steve Earle's song, *The Mountain*, which always compelled me to a place of awareness where surviving and moving forward were in and of themselves honorable and noteworthy achievements of a life. The new album was filled with songs like these, lyrics and melodies woven from hard-earned experience and rendered through voices of deep affection and cultural identity. They represented the best of how music mystically lifts our human spirit beyond the blemish of our natural condition. The fact that his voice was obviously strained from his cancer treatments drew me even closer to the music, because why would he pour so much of himself into something so strenuous, except for love?

The fact that we were both products of Arkansas predisposed me at an early age to follow his career. When *The Band* was at the center of the rock-n-roll movement in the 70s, I was a naïve teenager enchanted with visions of what the world should be, yet wholly unaware of what it would be. Raptured in the *Music from*

Big Pink, I bought my first guitar, a blonde Epiphone beauty with a laminated spruce top, straight maple sides and back, and an ebony fingerboard, at Cecil's Bandstand in Jackson, Tennessee for $375, a sizable investment for a 17-year old. Even more than the influence of his music, I most admired how Levon Helm's personality reflected his straightforward and authentic upbringing, like a man who easily recalled his youthful days picking cotton from the hard pack of Phillips County. Frequently, while listening to his music, my thoughts drifted to my grandparents, Oscar Peel and Ruth Blair, and the thickly wooded narrows from which their respective Scotch-Irish families fashioned their lives in northern Arkansas using the tools of strong backs and calloused hands. They were connected with the ground they tilled in ways our generation could not understand, a dirt that permeated every aspect of thought and action. They and the dirt were inseparable allies, as it was with so many who could remember drawing sustenance from the ground and not the grocery store. The soils of the hill country were sandy and thin, "*yeoman soil*" as my grandfather called it, where in order to survive your hands were as often on the gun as they were the plow. Levon's White River valley country was planter's soil, the alluvial lowlands rich in minerals and nutrients stolen from the mountain ranges in the glacial scrapping of the land, but equally demanding in the labor required to take anything from it. For both families, dirt meant life.

In Arkansas, dirt covered everything, got into everything, and meant everything. People sprang from it in their beginnings and returned to it at their endings. I stared at Levon's cover picture on the *Dirt Farmer* CD, he stooping down in a farmer's squat, a position that came as natural to him as a lion's crouch, boots tightened, soft eyes fixed toward tilled ground, and hard hands reaching out for the dirt that held the hidden words of his story. That picture was his testimony and my evidence of our shared humanity, a commonality of where we came from and where we so often longed to return. Once connected viscerally to the dirt, you could never leave it, and it would never leave you. I glanced out the window and noticed Kurt crossing the parking lot, shaking the cold from his winter coat. I thought about the dozens of trips that we took over the thirty years of our friendship, connecting ourselves to our own histories and the soil plowed by our immigrant ancestors. I knew that I was planted now in the dirt of my own life, living as a hibernating seed, incapable of fighting for myself and solely reliant upon the strength of others connected to me, where at the end of it I hoped to be found as faithful and authentic a man as the two men in my present company; one's orbit farther out and the other's closer in, but both drawn inextricably into the gravitational curve of my life.

"Trouble will snowball", Levon once said. *"The winds turn against you. Then you lose your faith"*. My joy left me over time, drip by drip, taking my faith with it until my bucket was emptied in abandonment. In light of tragedies that many others faced, the fate that befell me was perhaps not as horrific, not as worthy of sympathy or pity, not as deserving of compassion or aid, but when in the midst of great suffering of any kind, comparisons have no foothold. Great loss was all encompassing, not worthy of measurement and not to be segregated through any distinction, because to lose all one held most dear was to lose a heart's treasure, all of everything emptied out in merciless totality.

The Bible teaches that we often tumbled into holes that we dug for ourselves, sometimes in full knowledge of our rebellion, and other times unknowingly. In the reflection of the pain of those early weeks, I came to see that I had dug my own deep hole, never noticing the blisters from the shovel in my grip. It was the initial step, the initial point, of my way out, but I was months from knowing any healing. My life slipped from its moorings over the years as easily and painlessly as leaves falling from late autumn trees. All that was required was to turn my gaze away from what I treasured the most. After all, the heart nearly always follows the eyes. The change of my gaze was not sudden or abrupt. The deafening within my psyche occurred slowly over long stretches of time, like moss growing patiently on a rock until the day when its host is silently engulfed. As a tree bends to the weight of ice and snow throughout the storm and finally snaps, so was my long, dark winter.

Even as truths were revealed, I hesitated from turning from the accepted falsehood of the far more comfortable denials. Eventually, I would come to know, and know well, the full measure of the pain of truth, and the harshness of its reality. At the bottom, the real bottom, it was all I could do to hold onto my sanity. Everything seemed to fade into a great blackness, my orbit exposed to its generational patterns and weaknesses, with all ghosts returning to haunt me, taunting me with remindful jeers of far too many lessons learned only the hard way, and others never talked about, beneath shrouds of unperceived and unnoticed poor decisions.

Sitting at the table in Loveless Café, I was still motionless, deep inside of myself, as if staring up through some grand crevice in the earth, watching myself as perhaps God saw me, crawling along in my pity and not knowing how to climb into the light of freedom just ahead. Until that moment, I refused to talk about the specifics with anyone except God. Still, it was the music that spoke to me when all other voices could not, and it was Kurt's voice, the voice of my friend that answered my call, knowing me so well that as we spoke he did not need to be told that something was terribly wrong. As in the past and so many times before, his orbit would again join mine, his victories and sufferings would become my arsenal in the battle of healing, his friendship my *aide-de-camp*, the extension of his hand toward mine as a volunteer to the shared suffering that Christ-like love called us into. My friend stepped through the front door of Loveless Café.

Kurt's gotta know.

The line formed by these Water Tupelo trees in this headwater swamp face
due west and established the East-West baseline of the states later formed
from the Louisiana Purchase Territory. Blackton, Arkansas.

Chapter 1

« LAND OF OPPORTUNITY »

"Bring me men to match my mountains, bring me men to match my plains, men with empires in their purpose, and new eras in their brains." (Sam Walter Foss)

Obscurity often begins what ends in amazement, and so it was that in 1815 two parties of men set out on a very difficult journey. Working toward the same goal but headed in different directions, the land they were walking across was a wilderness with no trails or roads to guide them. Their tools were a compass, a 66' segmented chain, sextant and theodolite, instruments that assisted surveyors in measuring angles between fixed points and horizons. The first group led by surveyor Prospect Robbins began at the mouth of the Arkansas River where it joined the Mississippi in a location that today would be identified as the southeast corner of the state of Arkansas. He and a small crew of men headed due north, chopping and wading their way through the dense forest and lowland plains of the Louisiana Purchase's southern delta along a vertical line that would eventually end at the Canadian border and forever be identified as the Fifth Principal Meridian. In that same month of October, approximately one hundred miles to the northeast of the Robbins' group, a second surveying team set up camp at the convergence of the swampy St. Francis River and the Mississippi River.

Lead surveyor Joseph C. Brown and his small contingency of men headed west across brier thickets and mosquito filled swamps that scattered the landscape long before this part of the country was drained to expose its rich alluvial soil to agriculture. Brown's job was to strike the east-west baseline from where in time the boundaries of the future states of Arkansas, Missouri, Iowa, Minnesota, North Dakota, and part of South Dakota were fixed. In the cold winds of early November, the two parties crossed one another's line and marked a series of tupelo gum trees along a due west vector in a headwater swamp six miles west of the hamlet of Turkey Scratch, Arkansas. Adjacent to the *Witness Trees*, a lone granite marker stood in recognition of the Initial Point, the datum of the boundaries that established the 828,000 square miles that Thomas Jefferson bought from Napoleon Bonaparte in 1803 for $15 million USD. The purpose of the survey was to make good on a promise made by the United States government to the soldiers that served in the War of 1812: *"free land grants to those that serve."* The cash-strapped administration of James Madison needed new land to fulfill those promises, and the government encouraged settlers to move into the western territories under American impetus, our *Manifest Destiny*, but so as to also dissuade countries with any historical ties to the territory from attempting to assert or reassert their interests in the region, because settlers meant that militias could be formed, and settlements meant that forts could be built and supplied.

For over a century prior, a small colony had been established at the mouth of the confluence of the Arkansas and Mississippi rivers in 1686 by a French-speaking Italian fur trader named Henri de Tonti. By this date in 1815, the small French settlement of Arkansas Post consisted of a thriving and radically diverse river population numbering nearly two thousand souls. The survey work being undertaken by Robbins and Brown would enable the allocation of land with accuracy and legal mandate prior to the expected statehood of the Arkansas and Missouri territories, and our country could keep its word to the soldiers who fought for its freedom from Great Britain, my paternal ancestor James Carter

Hall among them. New horizons always attracted the most assertive people, and the corpse of this rich new territory was being skillfully prepared for the vultures of ambition and opportunism who would pursue their dreams of expansion, fame and fortune through early migration into the ancient lands of the Quapaw.

Within two years of the completion of the first three sections of the Louisiana Purchase survey, pioneers anxiously set about to elect their territorial Representatives. The subsequent First Territorial General Assembly convened in a tavern some sixty miles south of the Initial Point on July 28, 1819 at Arkansas Post along the 'Kicka' River. In the decade since the purchase of the territory, families eager to find new opportunities into cheap lands had begun pouring into the country well in advance of organized government and rule of law. Pioneers arrived by flatboat from the two main waterways that joined the Mississippi, moving along their tributaries and staking out farms up river from the Post. From the north and east, they came largely over land by way of the Southwest Trail, an old Indian path that began near Saint Louis, and stretched at a southwestern angle across the boundaries that now defined the state's borders, ending its southern terminus along the banks of the shallow and twisted Red River, the dividing line of Texas.

One of the first orders of business for the pioneers meeting at the Post was to decide upon a more centralized territorial capitol. Joab Hardin, Sr. was an early settler in the northern part of the territory who moved with a large group of families, our Peels among them, from Livingston County, Kentucky, the same year of the Robbins and Brown survey. They were fleeing the constant earthquakes of the New Madrid fault with land grants in hand. Hardin and his brother, Joseph, were elected by the small Cadron Settlement, which they helped establish, as its two Territorial Representatives. The Cadron Settlement sat high on a series of jagged bluffs along the Arkansas River in north-central Arkansas, modern day Faulkner County. The brothers fell to politics naturally, being a direct lineage from the Old Ben Hardin of

Bardstown Kentucky fame. They well understood the courtship of political power and personal fortune, and intended to use all possible influence to make Cadron Settlement the territory's first Capitol, and themselves rich and influential men as a consequence.

Immediately upon his arrival at Arkansas Post, Joab Hardin drafted and introduced a bill proposing Cadron as the Territorial Capitol. The bill received wide initial support from the small contingency of other legislators loosely scattered among the four corners of the territory, but equally intentioned counterforces began to rise in opposition, after powerful land speculator, William Russell, sent word from Saint Louis that an area south, and down river from Cadron, seemed a more suitable location for southern based trade. Traders and trappers called the place *"little rock"*, in reference to a small stone outcropping which breached the river's edge. Russell argued that the high bluff behind the landmark offered stronger natural defenses for a lasting settlement that could better defend itself against Indian infiltration. It was also widely known that Russell had staked his sizable fortune on the exploitation of the newly acquired territory and spared no expense in his philanthropy toward granting large tracts and select lots of his vast acreage to certain Territorial Representatives, the chief recipient of whom was Robert Crittenden, also a Kentucky transplant, the newly appointed and ruthlessly ambitious Territorial Secretary, who strongly rallied against the Hardin bill thereafter in alternative favor of Little Rock as the new territorial capitol. The Russell-Crittenden proposal prevailed in committee and several weeks later, upon the arrival of the Governor, was signed into law. The Hardin brothers had been trumped early at their own game of Kentucky poker, but the years ahead would provide them ample opportunity to play new hands.

The new Capitol of the southern Missouri Territory would be Little Rock, along the west bank of the Arkansas River, seven miles below Crystal Hill. Williams Russell's plan was underway. For years he had been purchasing transferrable land grant certificates, many bought at a substantial discount from veterans of the War of 1812, and others from settlers who claimed entitlement grants as a consequence of the New Madrid earthquakes. With the Territorial Secretary in his pocket, and now the Capitol in the heart of his land holdings, Russell was poised to become the king of this new kingdom. As an appropriate nod to its dubious land acquisition beginnings, directly across from the Arkansas State Capitol promenade in modern day Little Rock stands a modest, white stucco building which houses the Arkansas Board of Registration for Engineers and Land Surveyors; a permanent reminder of the inseparable partnership that the two factions have enjoyed since the state's very first political decision. On the large lawn of the state Capitol grounds, I played as a boy upon the neatly manicured grass that was once the site of the state's main penitentiary before its conversion into another type of criminal institution. As the afternoon sun set into the western sky on clear days, the impressive central dome, built from white Arkansas marble, casts a shadow that would almost reach to the backyard of my grandparent's house on South Pulaski Street.

I returned to Arkansas in 1980 to work in my family's food distribution business in the sweltering, southern border town of El Dorado. My wife and I were in our second year of marriage, trying to find our footing, locate steady work, and start a future together. I met Pam when she was a freshman at Austin Peay State University in Clarksville, Tennessee, just north of where her large family made their home in the township of Pond Switch at the western edge of Dickson County. Foolishly, I dropped out of college at the end of my sophomore year, set my back against the rolling hills of Tennessee, and headed west for what we hoped would be a new and better opportunity. My father nailed a thin metal sign over the battered warehouse of the fledgling new venture. Upon it was stenciled *"H & H Distributing Co."* across its center. A strange set of circumstances returned me to my birth state and into my father's dream of having his son work in the business; however, doing so would eventually break Pam's heart, and in that breaking, take mine with it. The day we pulled out in our Ford Pinto and U-Haul trailer she summoned the courage to encourage me forward, establishing a pattern that would repeat itself several times over the decades of our marriage. Like my ancestors generations earlier, we packed up what little we owned and chased the beckoning sun deep into the Land of Opportunity.

The Arkansas winter was just approaching but the temperatures were far milder than our experience in middle Tennessee. Gone were the soft rolling green hills and lush meadows of the Tennessee plateau, replaced with the thick, dreary pine forests stretched across the pancake land of southern Arkansas, where perpetually muddy creeks sifted out like molasses. Since the 1920s, wildcatters and corporate oil interests moved into this area to suck crude from tar deposits of the ancient Smackover Sea that flowed 1000 feet below the surface, and timber barons pillaged unlimited board feet of ancient forests, draining the swamps and clearing the land as they went, for the rice, cotton, and soybean fields that now stretched to the horizon.

My self-employed father owned a small wholesale food and fresh vegetable business, distributing to area schools, hospitals, and restaurants. The business sold locally grown tomatoes, imported Mexican cabbage, California leafy lettuce, fruits and green vegetables from Florida, as well as locally produced honey, butter, and cheese. We bought sweet onions by the tractor-trailer load from Georgia, and I delivered many sacks of these large gems to the local restaurants and area schools, which also included El Dorado's Sonic Drive-In, where we took pride in knowing that their special recipe onion rings were sourced from our stock. My father bought and sold hundreds of 25-lb sacks of *King Biscuit* flour and *Sonny Boy* corn meal from Helena's Interstate Grocery Company, and an equal number of bags of sugar from Ritchie Grocery in Texarkana. I made frequent trips to these wholesalers to pick up loads that we needed to fill orders because my father's business lacked the cash flow to hold sufficient inventories. At H & H Distributing, we became accustomed to *"robbing from Peter to pay Paul"* with money that was too often slow in coming back from customer receivables. The worst offenders were our government accounts, who normally ordered the most but paid us whenever they wanted to, daring us to say or do anything about it.

My parents lived in a well-kept neighborhood just south of town, not far from where the first production oil well had been drilled in 1920 that spurred the region's oil boom. Seeing active oil wells in this part of the country was a common occurrence, and there was one such pumping well located just outside of the front yard of my parent's home. The large rocker arm moved continuously up and down for the several years that my parents lived in that house, which drove my father to remind me at every opportunity, *"The bastard that owns that well just sits on his ass and waits for his check to show up."* The goosed-neck contraption also made a hideous buzzing-and-clink noise, constant and persistent, which caused the greatest irritation for my father, in particular. *"Bizz-clink-clink. Bizz-clink-clink."* Deposit the check. After months of constant complaining from my father and the other nearby neighbors, the subdivision developer reluctantly erected a wooden fence around the pumping ATM machine for aesthetic purposes, but the *"Bizz-clink-clink"* was hardly muffled, and the checks kept coming. Good work if you could get it.

Whether vast territory, timber, or mineral rights, the history of the state was filled with examples where outside interests moved in to take what they could and moved out to leave the cleaning up to the locals. Ingrained into the people that remained was a presumption of exploitation. Arkansans were well acquainted with lament. The real devils were the timber men and their clear-cutting. They raped the state of much of its foundational beauty. By most accounts, the oil industry scattered across the small towns of southern Arkansas resulted in more good for the people than bad, providing jobs where otherwise no jobs were available. The oil men were not saints by any measure, but they may have been the sole exception of the exploitation that seemed so often to repeat itself. Murphy Oil, to their credit, stuck it out with the people of Arkansas and meant more to the community of El Dorado than words could say. They were the best among a large cadre of the bad. *"Bizz-clink-clink." "Bizz-clink-clink."*

I learned quickly to loathe the giant mosquitoes, dirt silted creeks, and monotonous softwood forests around El Dorado, but there was something incredibly captivating about the vast spaces of open farmland and leftover scattered swamps that defined the area to the east, beyond the pine forests and out into the Arkansas delta. Despite the sparse population, our business drew a fair amount of trade throughout the region, and I looked forward to any excuse to find refuge in the delta on the days when my sales route or deliveries took me east toward the endpoints of the Arkansas and White rivers. Across the old plantations, ancient worker huts with rusted out corrugated tin roofs held together by overgrowth, still stood like discarded armor, dotting the fields along the narrow dirt access roads that drew squares around the row crops. Roads here took sudden, sharp turns at 90-degree angles in order to avoid crossing some farmer's crop line. The wide open land captivated me in a way that was not easily explained. It was organic. There was freedom inside the land's open arms, and I lost myself in the immensity of the horizons, like losing myself in a great book, or a lonesome song, and it was chasing after that same wandering and wonderment on the morning that first led me to the Louisiana Purchase Initial Point along Baseline Road in the corner of Lee, Phillips, and Monroe counties.

I left the house that morning before sunrise, as was my daily routine. After about an hour driving east, I caught the softening sky of the early morning light just beginning to glow over the curved horizon of the still dark earth. I was just outside of the little town of Hamburg, headed due east, when I first gazed upon the giant ball of yellow and white. In seconds, the sunrise broke the arch of the earth and radiated the land with a bath of colored light. The approaching warmth streaked the pale blue sky with faint wisps of gray and pink. I was so taken by the glorious site of the breaking dawn that I pulled over to the side of the road and stepped away from my vehicle. It was deathly quiet outside; not the kind of quiet that you feared, but the kind that embraced you. The vastness of the great space made me feel small, but certainly not insignificant. It felt as though God had brought the sun to me at just this moment and set it in the sky for my pleasure alone. It was breathtaking in its grandeur. Tears swelled up in my eyes as a wave of emotion overcame me. At the time, I could not recall seeing anything more beautiful.

Arkansas delta at sunrise, near Hamburg

The immense plain before me was cotton and rice country, where towers of grain bins stood from the ground like Sequoias silhouetted against the sky. As I scanned the broad open horizon, the emerging light ahead of me revealed pristine and perfectly plowed farmland in neatly combed cultivation lines. Curved water sprinkling equipment coated a light mist across a distant field, creating small rainbows in and among slivers of light. In those thousands of acres lay row after row of the source soil for much of the world's food and clothing supply, waiting patiently for the return of the warmer spring sun and the seed that would feed upon it. I pushed my face into the birthing rays of sunlight piercing the far horizon. The air passed cool through my nostrils and hinted of the musty soil around me. If I could have held the moment for a lifetime, I would have done so, but the life that I was yet to live, and the decisions that I would make to get there, waited for me farther down the road. I did not know then as a young man what I do know now as an old man; that moments of bliss never last. They sweep randomly across our fate for brief instances of time, to be cherished in memory as much as in experience.

Watching the sun lift itself over the distant tree line, my thoughts were captured by what had quickly become a situational nightmare for me and my new bride. A tough and early major life decision was upon me, and one that felt far beyond my youthful years to make. I was not yet qualified for manhood. The business was struggling, and my Dad's troubles from his earlier involvement with Valley Institutional Products, Inc., based in Pine Bluff, stalked him down to El Dorado, where he had hoped to start over. The federal authorities showed up at the door of my parent's home one evening, asking a lot of questions about the business practices of VIP Foods. Prior to H & H Distributing, my father was one of the owners and executives of the thriving, regional food distribution company. The same practices that concerned the FBI had also concerned my Dad, enough so that he sold his interest in VIP Foods, gathered up his life savings, and bought a fledgling food distributorship based in El Dorado that he named "H & H Distributing." Years of trouble followed my father from that day forward until his death, although I watched him do everything he could do to avoid it. It was a fearful thing to consider, making a single bad decision that could burden your life for so long. My mother was never easy to live with, or work with, long before the troubles of VIP, but this new set of events pushed her over her emotional edge. Now, within four months of our move away from Tennessee, Pam and I found ourselves lost in a swirl of conflict not of our own making.

In a fit of rage driven no doubt from my mother's accumulated stress and fears, she fired Pam from the office and announced to me upon my arrival back from my sales route that my wife was no longer a part of the family business. My Dad, already bending to the bleakness of his legal situation, could not find the will to undue the betrayal. Pam had left the company and was now working as a technician at a local hospital, but everything had changed. The dream my dad and I shared had died. My parents seemed to live in the expectation that this decision would have no consequences, but I knew from the moment it happened that Pam and I must move on, and I also knew that moving on would break my Dad's heart.

A quick burst of cool air blew across my face and snapped me back into the present reality of the grand sunrise before me. My eyes were drawn toward a string of ducks flying directly overhead, forming their V-shaped vector which acted like an arrow, guiding their migration journey across a hazel sky. Each duck in the chain took its turn as the leader, and then voluntarily fell back, as another took its place. I could see in the distance other strings of migrating birds converging upon that same flight corridor. The sun was moving rapidly away from the horizon line where it first escaped the darkness only moments earlier. I could faintly make out the distant and haunting cry of the ducks as they cut a wedge through the high air. Toward the north, closer in, another group formed into a swirling cone, like the shape of a tornado, in what could only be described as a ballet of twirling movement, an ethereal dance. The ducks individually swirled around one another in elegant grace and at regular intervals dropped out of the bottom of the funnel and landed onto the dew covered ground below. In a few brief seconds, all of the ducks that formed the original cone landed safely onto the cut fields. There was a wonderful sense of calm in their order and dignity, and I burst into tears with emotions no longer willing to hide.

The stop along the road gave me a few moments of peace that I so deeply and desperately craved. I pulled back onto the highway and headed toward my first customer farther north in DeWitt at Rice Belt Vo-Tech. Meredith Gresham, a woman of divine spirit and alleged granddaughter to the legendary blues harp virtuoso, Sonny Boy Williamson, was the food buyer for the school, and she always offered me a couple of their fresh baked cookies as a traveling snack. From her example I learned that kindness only needed the smallest of offerings to reveal itself, and I was counting on that kindness and those cookies upon my arrival. From the school, there were calls to make in Stuttgart, Claredon, DeValls Bluff, and Brinkley, after which I normally backtracked through Pine Bluff on my way home, ostensibly doing some prospecting during my return trip. Today would need to be different. I felt a calling to head east and make the required contacts on my inbound trip rather than my outbound. I had ventured a different return route on a couple of occasions and this day seemed perfect for a similar detour. After Rice Belt Vo-Tech, I would proceed east, across the White River into Marvel, then head north to Brinkley, passing near Levon's boyhood home of Turkey Scratch along the way. Maybe I could find time to stop for a hand-cut bologna sandwich and Mountain Dew at A. B. Thompsons for an early lunch. Just the thought of it drove me forward into temporary disavowal of my reality. These were in fact long days away from Pam with no way to contact her but there would be longer ones ahead for both of us. As much as I so badly wanted to live in the future, it was good that God granted us only the present.

Tire Man, Dumas, Arkansas

"THIS STONE MARKS THE BASE ESTABLISHED NOVEMBER 10, 1815 FROM WHICH THE LANDS OF THE LOUISIANA PURCHASE WERE SURVEYED BY UNITED STATES ENGINEERS. THE FIRST SURVEY FROM THIS POINT WAS MADE TO SATISFY THE CLAIMS OF THE SOILDERS OF THE WAR OF 1812 WITH LAND BOUNTIES. ERECTED BY THE ARKANSAS DAUGHTERS OF THE AMERICAN REVOLUTION. SPONSORED BY THE LANGUILLE CHAPTER."

Chapter 2

« INITIAL POINT »

To be a part of a family run business really means that whatever needs to be done, you get to do it. When I wasn't loading trucks or making deliveries, I was peddling fresh and canned food to our restaurant, small store, and public school customers across the region. I bore the burden of being a young man with little experience and a wandering mind, filled with dreams of what I hoped to be, but stuck in the reality of who I was. As a means of fulfilling my wanderlust, I would purposely vary my travels along my sales and delivery routes, exploring any available opportunity to entertain my mind while not revealing my travel transgressions to management, i.e., my father. There were no cellular telephones in those days, so finding me after I left the business was nearly impossible, and catching me in my wanderings equally as difficult, unless I missed an expected delivery or sales call, prompting the customer to call the office. It was hard to judge whether these frequent side attractions were motivated more in my intellectual curiosity or in task avoidance, and in my case, I irrefutably suffered from both maladies. As I drove along the empty highway headed toward DeWitt, I checked the folded state map in search of an alternative exploratory route to Brinkley. From the map, I saw that following AR#1 would hook me up with US#49 with little noticeable delay. Tracing the lines of those highways across the wrinkled map surface with my eyes, I detected the notation of *Louisiana Purchase Historical Marker* in small red print just east of my newly committed journey. I had seen the notation before but not given it thoughtful notice; however, on this day I was looking for a needed distraction from my troubles, and the marker label intrigued me.

I arrived at the park's nondescript entrance about 8:30 a.m., where a long and straight gravel-packed road greeted me toward a remote parking lot that dead-ended into a swamped forest grove. The place was deserted and looked almost abandoned. I stepped out of my vehicle, slipped on my jacket to offset the chill, and walked along the raised berm that separated two lower areas where dark water collected on either side. The uncut, wet Fescue left water stains and tiny grass seedlings clinging to my shoes. A crow sounded his lonely cry from somewhere deep among the thicket. The air was damp and cold inside the grand stand of tupelo and cypress trees, as the mild temperature of the morning felt like it had dropped twenty degrees inside the forest lair. Ancient waterborne trees established random lines in all directions, tall and erect throughout the grove, like soldiers at morning muster. It was eerie and alluring, so beautiful in its uniqueness that I was drawn to its wonder, but fearful of its unknown.

Across the parking lot, I noticed a planked path that snaked itself deeper into the woods. Stomping on the parking lot pavement to remove the water and grass from my shoes, I proceeded along the staggered boardwalk and into the forest. The winding, planked footpath, like a maze of trees, twisted directions so many times that I had no idea in what direction I was walking. I stopped and gave myself a minute to become more at ease with the silence and the uncanny stillness of the place. I cinched up the zipper on my jacket and tried to calm my senses, determined to embrace its remoteness rather than fear it. I took a slow, deep breath. The subtle sounds coming from the swamp were like magical notes bouncing around in the air. There was nothing here to fear, but much to honor. Nature still ruled herself in this holy place, and here, hidden from the rest of the world, she was untouched, still powerful and wild.

It was rare in my life that I was this far away from noise, and while initially disconcerting, continued exposure to the silence calmed my senses, sharpening them to the sounds and small movements of the headwater swamp and the creatures that lived in it. The birds chirped distinctly in each of their individual songs. They darted from tree to tree like fairies. A random red-tailed squirrel scurried about and barked at my interruption of his morning foraging. Frogs moved from their sunning locations as the noise of my footsteps along the planked walkway took to their notice, each time flopping into the murky water with a *"blurp"*. Along the trenched areas in the swamp, a thick layer of green slime and black syrup surrounded thousands of fallen leaves that had piled during the winter and deteriorated into a soft, yucky muck.

I moved ever deeper into the gum thicket along the pathway, passing the watchful eyes of the noble trees and straining for views of the surrounding fields between hundreds of white ashen trunks. Suddenly, I came upon a large stone marker standing alone in the middle of the swamp like a lost child. The roughhewn granite base, which I guessed to be about a foot deep, was swallowed up almost completely by the black-and-green muck. It was as if the great rock had been hurled from an asteroid belt, set loose from the rings of Saturn, and dropped from the sky to settle here, unknown to anyone but God. This place was so remote that surely the people that built it had forgotten that it ever existed. The stamped bronze inscription offset into the stone noted this location as being the starting point for the surveying of the lands of the Louisiana Purchase. The boundaries for six states would eventually be marked based upon the coordinates of this Initial Point established by two surveyors on November 10, 1815. Two gum trees still bore the faded scars of the markings of Robbins and Brown.

1926 dedication of the Historical Marker of the Initial Point for the survey of the Louisiana Purchase. Thaddeus and Hattie Caraway are circled.

The tall cypress trees around me swayed and creaked as the prairie wind rushed through their tops. The wide and lumpy roots of the Tupelos reached deep into the loose peat, their finger-like branches filtering the winter sun's warming rays. Headwater swamps like this one were a treasured rarity, all but eliminated by the unabated expansion of farming land acquired by draining the basins and clearing the forest from the plains. They appeared periodically across the barren landscape in areas where water normally pooled but with volumes too low to accumulate into a pond or lake. Most people that looked out across these miles of fields rarely considered how the land looked before the axe and the saw chopped away all the timber, pulled up all the briers, and turned the once heavily forested thickets into plowed rows. The few remaining swamps and troughs were natural cooling centers from summer's heat, and places to hold sacred. They were hidden in pockets along the miles of irrigation canals and small streams that crisscrossed the triangulated land, impossible to find except to seekers.

The rare groves of ancient swamp trees, which through the protection of the gods and oversight from loggers, not uprooted and sawed into board, offered up their own natural air conditioning. The more shrewd flatlanders across the decades wisely planted their homes near these cool pools, where they enjoyed a renewing respite from the pounding heat of the long Arkansas summers. The mosquitos that made these lairs their home were another topic. The gum grove and scattered cypress trees around the marker stood as thick as hairs on a dog's back, and I had difficulty seeing a far point more than a dozen yards in any direction. A sign posted by the Park Service pointed out the pure westward alignment of a set of gum trees that seemed to me should have been pointing due north. Pondering about the lonely stone, I seemed a thousand miles away from anywhere and could not have felt more isolated from the stresses of the world outside these boundaries. This remote spot of earth had surely changed little since 1926, when the monument was officially dedicated during an extended dry period which allowed a wagon to haul the granite marker to its final resting place. The small group of local officials were joined by officers of the Daughters of the American Revolution, and the well-known Arkansas State Senator from Jonesboro, Thaddeus H. Caraway, and his wife Hattie, who had ventured here wearing their Sunday finest; he in a double-breasted dark suit and she sporting a new bonnet. The local chapter of the DAR was comprised of ladies mainly from the nearby towns of Marianna and Brinkley. Two young children dressed as English pygmies rounded out the historical presentation.

I stood for several minutes more in the mist of the brisk air surrounded by aged and stately trees, staring blankly at the cold stone monument, waiting perhaps for it to make a movement or a sound, but it did not. In the peaceful silence I thought about my Dad, about my new wife, about what might happen to us, about what I knew I had to do, and just how much I dreaded doing it. A part of me wished that I could sink into the swamp muck and disappear from the fear and dread. I dreamed of being carried off to a magical land of limited responsibilities and no major decisions, which prior to my marriage, was the land of my existence. I was twenty-two years old and had greatly resisted growing up, but in the cold shade of the tree blanket, I realized that this time fate would not leave me untested as a man, as a son, and mostly as a husband. For myself I felt sorrow but my heart broke in two for Pam. How lonely she must feel, so far away from her home and among only my family, who had set her outside of their caring. None of this was her doing. Slowly and regretfully, I eased back to my car, along the way admiring the longevity and peacefulness of this inexplicably beautiful tiny point on the map, nearly hidden in obscurity among the vast fields of the Arkansas delta and the White River bottomlands. The small forest remained so constant to its original creation, unspoiled by the forces of the world that surrounded it, and unaware of the combustion of cities and towns spawned from its anchor point.

Like a single match that started a forest fire, it had no idea of the size of the blaze it sparked. Multiples of thousands of people lived upon plots of land that were referenced against this exact location, those two marked trees, and people did not know they even existed. So like so many things of human ignorance, once built, assumed to have always been there, with few taking the time to praise the effort that created it. All things good had a worthy beginning, but we became so accustomed to taking so much for granted that we often forgot that axiom. The marked trees were like a great force that went about their invisible work in silence, seeking no acclaim, with the deep significance of their faithfulness revealed only in reference to subsequent accomplishments. I bemoaned that the great stone had not the power to return me to an earlier time and redirect the vectors of fate that spilled into the pathway of my young life. Across the ensuing years, facts bore out that forgiving was much easier than forgetting, or maybe the forgiveness was not perfected until the forgetting was. Reaching the parking lot, I paused for a last look around, realizing that I was looking at a seed that yielded a continent, and that thought made me smile in awe of it. I wondered to myself, when, if ever, I would return, and where my life would be when I did. Exiting along the narrow access road, I passed the raised berm, black water, and stands of stalwart trees which gave their leave to the open fields of rich soil and irrigation ditches ahead. I knew that soon I would be leaving Arkansas for a second time, and saying goodbye again to the land and dirt of my birth.

Original building of H & H Distributing Co., El Dorado, Arkansas

Chapter 3

« TROUBLE WILLL SNOWBALL »

Winter crept up on me like a thief and the bitter cold morning forced me to notice it. I pulled out my heavy Carhartt from the back seat of my truck, tossed it on, and walked across the broad parking lot and up the wooden steps into the small white building just off of Highway 70 in west Nashville. It was warm inside and the restaurant chatter made me fell welcomed. The hostess led me to a small side table where I could see the parkway out the window. The table was covered with a traditional red checkered tablecloth, the same pattern that I recognized from the occasional breakfast with my dad at the local diner in Brownsville before one of our fishing trips. My lifelong friend, Kurt Beasley, agreed to meet me this morning at Loveless Cafe, neither of us actually putting together the irony of the name of the business given my present state of mind. Our friendship dated back thirty years, before Kurt finished law school and me business school, before we each had three children, and back to when we were both paying for our first home purchases. My wife Pam had known Kurt and Teresa Beasley since grade school. Growing up together in Dickson County, Tennessee, their families were faithful members of Dickson First Baptist Church. Few secrets existed between Kurt and me, but I had held onto one for months without telling him. We first met at church, not long after Pam and I returned from Arkansas where I had left our family business. On a hot July day, Kurt and I built a fence together across his back patio. The fence was eventually torn down but our friendship still stood. I liked him from the first minute we met. His manner incorporated humor into every life event, no matter how tragic, and his humor had encouraged me through good times and bad times. We were brothers in every sense except shared blood. He and I loved this small café, renowned for its freshly baked biscuits and homemade jams. The superb reputation of the famous café, located near the northern terminal point of the Natchez Trace Parkway, had been faithfully earned over the years. After checking in with him during a brief conversation a few days earlier, Kurt sensed something amiss and suggested that we meet this morning for breakfast. We had always been there for each other, one helping the other in times when the sense of life turned senseless. This was one of those times.

Loveless Café' near Natchez Trace Parkway, Bellevue, Tennessee

A couple of days earlier, I stopped at the record store and picked up a copy of Levon Helm's *Dirt Farmer* CD as a belated Christmas gift for Kurt. The holiday season had passed me by with little celebration. While I waited for him to arrive, I glanced through the liner notes and sipped on a hot cup of coffee that the waitress assumed I needed without request. At her almost every pass she splashed in a few more ounces to top off my mug, unintentionally interrupting my wandering thoughts. I felt the sense of anticipation that was common when waiting for a dear friend and knowing that some of the shades of my sadness would be pushed aside, if only temporarily. Kurt would find something to make fun of but better to laugh occasionally than to cry constantly.

My friend was no stranger to feelings of loss. He lost his older brother, Darrell, to cancer when Kurt had not yet finished high school. An automobile accident left his middle brother committed to an institutional life of care due to brain trauma as an adult. Both brothers were brilliant and handsome, the older having established himself as a young marketing executive, and the middle brother as a widely heralded physician. I watched my friend bear these hardships with much grace, his own fortress built from the bricks of his deep personal faith in Christ and a sense of Christian responsibility that was drummed into his psyche by his father and mother, their lives equally committed to the ministry in service of small church communities across southern Missouri and western Tennessee.

Kurt's father was one of the last of the circuit riding preachers except that his transportation was an old car instead of a horse, and he dragged his entire family along from church to church on Sundays, where Kurt and his brothers spent hours away from television, dressed in their Sunday best, trying not to fall asleep in the middle of their father's multiple, similar sermons. Few pastors today were left to commit so much hard work for so little reward. Through year after year of toil inside of Freewill Baptist churches with no more than fifty members, the efforts of Pastor Hildon and Virginia Beasley may have seemed insignificant in light of the size of the churches they led, but it was their service to others that established the legacy that continued through their influential youngest son and the hundreds of other people that benefited from knowing them and witnessing their faithful service. In no small way, the hands of my friend, joined with his wife Teresa, were now extending the work of his parents, touching more lives than Pastor and Mrs. Beasley could have imagined. It was never more apparent to me than in Kurt's life the exponential curve of good works, reminding us that whatever our efforts, whatever our calling, we should not try and measure its results. The grace we seek was found in the love of the doing.

The faithful circuit pastor was buried in the small community of Erin, Tennessee, a parcel of rolling wetlands landlocked at the base of the Land between the Lakes where the Tennessee River and Cumberland River formed the two great lakes of Kentucky and Barkley, respectively. It was a beautiful area, still maintained by a predominantly evangelical community that somehow managed to stay here and had not been forced to leave in order to secure a more reliable income. Lush in vegetation and timber, the area remained relatively obscured from modern life. The railroad had bypassed the town in favor of a Waverly hub which provided a straighter line to the Tennessee River from its Kingston Springs connection point, and there was no passageway out of town other than to the south. His father pastored small churches throughout the territorial cul-de-sac from Dickson to Tennessee Ridge in the later years of his active life. Brother Shorty put some serious miles on that old Ford, nodding off at the wheel at regular intervals, fighting against his narcolepsy until the end, with cigar in hand (only for chewing) and terrified family in tow.

Kurt was with me to bury my father in Little Rock, and I was with him to bury his father in Erin, two days that neither of us imagined would be as hard as they were. I remember vividly the day of Pastor Beasley's funeral, as before that day, I did not truly realized the extent of the character and talents of the Beasley family, and the array of successful and purposeful people that comprised it. At the funeral home, on a small table in the vestibule, the family placed a few of Pastor Beasley's personal items for review. As I thumbed through the mementoes of his life's work, which included his ragged personal King James Bible, I also noticed a well-worn paperback book titled, *A Treatise of the National Association of Freewill Baptists*, published by the association's Nashville-based publishing entity, Randall House. It was less than a year since my visit to Randall House Publishing to meet with its soon to be retiring Chief Executive Officer, Alton Loveless. I was there to congratulate Dr. Loveless, my cousin, on his forthcoming retirement and to discuss some specifics around an ongoing genealogical project that had peaked his interest for years. An accomplished traveler and genealogist, Alton first captured my attention in the late 1990s, when I noticed a posting that he made on the internet on behalf of the Blair family, my grandmother's line in northern Arkansas. His posting included my name and the names of my sisters in the expanded tree of Blair's, who dated back to an arrival in America through the port of Savannah by William Hiram Blair *circa* 1750. At that time, I was surprised to find that I had a cousin so deeply accomplished and admired in his life's work. Now, looking down at a book published while my cousin was managing Randall House, held and cherished by Kurt's father, I could see his fingerprints alongside of Pastor Beasley's, both men true to their own calling in service to their Lord and connected to one another through their silent labors. Their linked history was not unlike the initial friendship that was formed when Kurt and I labored together on his fence more than thirty years ago, still building lives that intertwined in ways incomprehensible to imagine had we not had each other to depend upon.

During the funeral of Pastor Beasley, there were no discussions about his ecumenical viewpoint, or the specifics of his denominational doctrine as a Freewill Baptist. Rather, all memories about the pastor's life were of his service to others, the relationships that he built and cherished along his life's journey, and the humorous stories that made his story uniquely his own. Given the wide disparity of beliefs and denominations represented in that room, all thought of theological ideas and precepts slipped into a vast obscurity, and what remained of his life were remembrances of the work done, the goodness shared, and the kindness given. I wondered in reflection of that experience why so many faiths worked so hard to find reasons to keep people out, to keep people away from one another, when at the end, when all else was peeled away, the theology meant so little in comparison to the shared humanity of the life lived. I knew in ways that few others did how closely my friend Kurt was honoring the legacy of his itinerant preaching father, even though he would be more than reluctant to admit it. Kurt committed his time and talents toward a number of charitable and faith-based works, numerous mission trips to foreign lands, many of them dangerous, and countless hours of free legal work and unpaid consultation for the inherent benefit of the labors of those outreach enterprises. It was the same work as his father, accomplished under a different label but with equal tenacity.

I carefully creased the liner notes of *Dirt Farmer* and slipped the small booklet back into the jewel case. Out the cafe window, I noticed Kurt jogging across the parking lot, whipping at his overcoat and straining against the cold toward the front door of the restaurant. I thought about how, in Levon's life, grace had come back to him when all else looked like a disaster. He held on until the winds changed their direction. This CD was evidence. I thought about my friend Kurt, how much he had endured, and was still enduring, but willing yet to make room to share my burdens as well. Bearing out suffering in faith was a form of courage too little noticed. Things moved to bad, and then slipped into worse, but eventually time would lift the load, a path and pattern that life seemed determined to enforce upon us, as we praised during the highs and learned during the lows. In the center of that place where the darkness was most complete, a small sliver of light beamed back onto my soul, and my cell phone lit up, my friend answered, and I was here, still in the process of relearning who I was and what really mattered when the rest was swept away.

I recalled that I once read C. S. Lewis stating that life experience was the *"harshest of all taskmasters."* In my own life, I often wished to gain the knowledge which came through experience without having endured the experience that yielded the knowledge. I remembered from a book read years ago that Robert Kennedy turned to Aeschylus for comfort at the deaths of his brother, John, and his friend, Martin Luther King, Jr. With a wisdom that transcended the poet's human perspective, he proclaimed, "*For it was Zeus who set men on the path to wisdom when he decreed the fixed law that suffering alone shall be their teacher. We learn unwillingly. From the high bench of the gods by violence, it seems, grace comes.*" I brushed a tear aside and prayed that such grace would find me again, and I looked up, greeted my friend, and slid Levon's CD across the table.

Chapter 4

« THE HONEY BEE »

Aaron left for boot camp on a rainy Monday evening in mid-March. Pam and I dropped him off at the hotel near downtown Nashville, and I hugged my son knowing that such opportunities would be few over the next several years, fully cognizant of the unknowns in life that had befallen me many years earlier when I had a similar parting with my own father. The history of my experience with my Dad had circled around to haunt my present. After working without interruption since I was sixteen years old, and on top of the rest of my troubles, I was fired from my first job at fifty. In the case of Aaron and me, I did not want our relationship to suffer from my failures in the same way that mine did with my father. I knew instinctively at the time that his mother and I were saying goodbye to a boy and would welcome back a man. And that's what happened. For Aaron, joining the Navy was clearly the right move and over time his service proved to be a positive experience in his life, albeit not without a few bumps along the way. On the night of his parting, the good that was yet to come could not be foreseen as Pam and I drove home in the rain feeling the full weight of his decision and its effects. I felt so guilty, having to face the truth that our current failings left us with so little else to offer him, and now his course was set and could not be reversed. Several weeks later without hearing a word from him otherwise, the single traditional "1st letter home" arrived, written in his unmistakable horrible handwriting. The brief note was scratched out in pencil, barely discernible and not encouraging. It read: *"Mom and Dad I won't lie. It's hell here.*

They treat us like dogs. I hate it. I hate this place. I hope you and the animals are doing OK. Say 'Hi' to the family. Your son, Aaron."

As Aaron struggled through boot camp, I watched my life in Tennessee, day after day, slip past sympathetic tragedy into absurd comedy, refusing any remote thought that I could somehow control the rate of its descent. Near the bottom of the pile, I found an unusual peace in the clear recognition that, at this point in my life, I had absolutely no effect on the outcomes of my fate. Even more profound lessons would be found in the pit of failure. I was learning how to let go of everything that I had come to believe defined me, mostly because it was ripped out of my proud hands. I was seeing the world more in its truth than its sales pitch. The well-constructed life that I once embodied had vanished. I felt the freedom of refusing to own the shame of multiple failures, opinions served up by others, perhaps well-intentioned, but from people equally as guilty of some hidden or unspoken failure of their own. The process of this purging totally exposed my inadequacies and left me singularly as the insecure, hurting, and uncertain man that I had worked so hard to keep hidden away. It took sweeping everything out in order to find a new way, a common journey, but unique to my experience. It was a lesson that I could have more easily learned through different means, but life seemed to give us the medicine that we needed the most and desired the least, and in appropriate doses. In time, I would see that at the place I least expected, at bedrock bottom of my life, in ruins and among the tares, I met my faith face to face again; and it was good, and merciful, and holy. It was so simple a lesson it seemed embarrassing now in its simplicity, but I came to fully understand that I was a single, uniquely created but flawed human, and that I owned no other life but mine. I owed that life a promise to not live it to the expectations of others. I owed that life a break.

In my newfound solitude, my thoughts would drift back to that cold February day almost thirty years earlier in El Dorado, standing on the loading dock of our old tin-roofed building with my father at 5:00 a.m., where I told him that I was moving back to Tennessee, quitting the business, and leaving Arkansas. Filled with an idealism that life had no intention of delivering, I watched as the tears rolled down my father's face in random streams. The sun had not yet risen, and we spoke in the dimness of the dock lights that were strung across the loose tin roofing. Nobody was stirring on that early morning, and even the softness of our voices carried into the parking lot and out across the railroad tracks. I could not bear to look at him for more than a few seconds at a time, as it was too painful. Drawing his handkerchief from his back pocket, in a broken voice he glanced up at me, *"You should stay, son. I don't want you to leave. How will I do this without you?"* I kicked my work boot against one of the metal poles on the dock and the bell-like sound echoed into the crisp morning air. I jammed my hands into my coat pockets. *"I can't Dad. I just can't."* After a few seconds, he wiped his face and nodded his head in silent resolve, and then he turned and walked away. All the while I wanted to tear my heart out of my chest, but I felt that I had no other moves. My family was Pam. Although time would prove how horribly I would mismanage my future relationship with her, I cut the cord between my parents and me that morning and embraced my new life with my new wife. I look back at it all now with an understanding that I never want a moment of parting ways like that with my own son, and with God's grace, will never have one.

Three decades passed by like turning pages in a book, and the years of time that separated the failings of my father's poor decisions were now echoing in my life, as if two bound lives in separate orbits. As Levon had said, sometimes the winds will turn against you. I felt firsthand how my Dad felt then; enduring the irreplaceable emptiness, falling and falling into a void, not catching the hint of a break, and begging to wake up from the nightmare. At twenty-six years old, I watched my father die as a broken man. I am sure that he felt like a failure although none of us that loved him believed he was. We never spoke of what he learned in the descent, but I had an idea of it. I also believed that God was going to give me a chance to find and know myself, particularly if I paid attention during the climb out. What I could not have imagined was the object that would be the source of the spark that initiated my turning point.

At the point where I embraced the unknown outcome of my fate, in an unremarkable moment of solitude while sitting at home alone, I heard a buzzing sound of a wayward honey bee. It was late April, and plants were flowering, bees were swarming, and the sun was coming up earlier and staying around longer. As the small bee moved from room to room, I could hear its buzzing, and its body bumping up against the window glass. It remains a mystery to me why the bee suddenly garnered so much of my attention. I have concluded in retrospect that God decided that my own descent had lasted long enough, and it was time that I woke up, got up off of the couch, quit feeling sorry for myself, and return to the world. The small insect flew past me two or three times, as I continued to watch and listen, but made no movement. Suddenly and instantly, my eyes opened again to the stimuli of the outside world. Colors not before noticed rushed into view. The hairs on my arm tingled with electricity, and the weight that was sitting on my chest for months, inextricably lifted from me. I breathed in the freshness of the fragrant air that was flooding into our home through the screen door. Its sweet, subtle aroma hinted of honeysuckle, and reminded me of my days as a boy searching for muscadines among the vacant land near my North Little Rock home. I rose from the couch and stepped out onto the front porch, and felt the sun on my face, and heard the birds singing, and wondered where I had been for so long.

How the bee found entry into our home also remained a grand mystery. In its foraging, it had perhaps found a crack or crevasse too well hidden to return to for escape. I crept toward the creature for a closer examination and noticed that the bee looked typical of the species that I was familiar with in this area of the country. About the size of my thumbnail, it bore a yellowish-brown torso with zebra-like black stripes across its body. I realized that this time of year, with the flowers in early bloom, that the bee was on a mission of finding nectar for its hive, or scouting a safe place for a queen to build one. Honey bees are normally very docile unless adversely provoked, and I had no intention of provoking my new friend. My thoughts went straight to our son Aaron, who was aboard a naval destroyer heading toward the Panama Canal. As a child, he was known in the family as the *"bee charmer"* because on more than one occasion he brought in a honey bee on his finger for us to see, having gently coaxed it away from the honeysuckle and flowers in our backyard. His gentle nature being no threat to the bees, we saw no reason as parents to prevent him from these encounters. We would watch him often following a bee from flower to flower with his index finger extended toward it in innocent invitation. He was never stung in these encounters. Nature knew that reaching out in love was never to be feared.

I followed the bee from room to room, carefully watching her fly from here to there throughout the house so as not to impede her determined search for an escape route. I went to the back door and swung it open, pinning the brace mechanism against the retriever so that the door would hold itself, creating what I hoped would be an obvious path to freedom. A chance occurrence, perhaps, of her captivity would provide me an opportunity to assist with her freedom. Or, did she find me through divine design, a small friend sent to renew my senses, and beckon me back into the fullness of my available joy? I started thinking about how much I enjoyed honey, and how hard that single bee was working on behalf of the hive to collect the nectar that would eventually become the honey that I loved so much. My mind recalled a documentary film on bees that I watched some time earlier on public television, highlighting many of the amazing characteristics of their society. Here was one of its faithful representatives, doing the work for which she was compelled by forces that she did not understand, volunteering her service to God and inside of the majesty of His design. Driven by her natural instincts, the bee must have been temporarily disconnected from her calling and became trapped, but with help from a power beyond her own capabilities, a path to freedom could be found. The parallel metaphor of her life and mine did not escape my notice. I determined in that instant to help her with all my might.

I began my freedom quest by making my presence known to the bee, standing in the doorways and in front of the windows, hoping that I could directionally compel her flight toward the open back door. The bee was ever persistent in her search for escape, flying into anything and anywhere that drew in the outside light, except the open door, which seemed impossible for her to find. From room to room with arms outstretched I chased after the buzzing bee, stepping into and away from her flight path, and shouting, *"Free yourself!"* at the top of my lungs. Noticing my own antics made a smile come to my face and an unusual sense of joy swelled up in resulting emotion. I laughed uncontrollably and exuberantly. I yelled, *"Fly! Fly bee! Fly away!"*, and didn't care who heard me. Time after time the bee would pass near the open back door, but would not exit. Tiring from my initial efforts, I sat back onto the sofa and watched the poor creature move from room to room, window to window, banging her body against what she believed to be a route to freedom. How long would this futility last? And in the moment of that thought, I recognized my own life and God's view of it. In the bee's erratic desperation I saw my own reckless efforts to try and free myself, not noticing that God was right there all the time, holding the door open, waving His hands, and screaming at the top of His lungs, *"Free yourself, Kenny! Fly to freedom! Kenny, be free!"* Swelling tears acknowledged His guiding Spirit and my recognition of His voice. The bee's freedom was my freedom and the turn away from our shared suffering became my determined promise.

I jumped from the couch, fetched a broom from the closet and grabbed a notepad from my desk. As gently and deliberately as possible, I crept from room to room with broom and notepad in hand, moving to and fro, trying to coax the bee to freedom. I made no sudden gestures to incur her anger or provoke her fear. My concern for the bee's well-being drew me into close proximity on more than one occasion, closer to her potential sting than comfortable distance would afford me, but I fought back any fear of being stung and set my mind on the purpose at hand. I had to admit, however, that freeing her was requiring sizable effort. She flew from eve to eve and room to room, again passing by the open door without turning, and in repetition, I mercifully extended broom and notepad, alternating notepad and broom, together and independently, in constant sway. I spent the better part of fifteen minutes running through the house in a dance of freedom with the bee, inspiring her with my words and movements, encouraging her toward the light. Finally, without fanfare or apparent significance, the bee abruptly turned through the open door to the outside, and simply flew away. She was free again, and so was I.

Drawn to follow her movements as far as possible, I stepped outside onto the deck and traced her path with my eyes until she disappeared into the woods that lined the back of our property. All of my senses tingled with new energy. I knew instinctively that in just a matter of minutes the bee would be reunited with her hive and then back again foraging for nectar in service of the queen, wholly putting this misadventure behind her. Bees live in the moment and do not dwell obsessively over their past. There was too much work to be done. What wisdom creation reveals when we are listening and watching.

I had otherwise dwelt on the past without ever realizing until that moment just how trapped I was inside of my own house, a hive built with my own hands while my wife and children were forced to stand outside of its boundaries and watch the project, brick by brick, year after year, closing myself up to them while burying myself in my work, the easy part for me, and how I pursued it with such passion and commitment. I never remembered asking Pam or the children if they considered the sacrifice of my time and involvement for my career as being worth it. I considered it worth it, and so by default, expected them to feel accordingly. I was devastated the day that Pam and I walked into our back field and sat down in the high grass, where she told me that I had been gone for so long that she had learned not to need me. I had become almost a stranger to the person whose singular love I was completely reliant upon. I couldn't believe what I was hearing, but there it was, and even then, I denied its reality. The house I had labored on for so long only had room enough for one when it was completed, and I was lost inside of it. Droning on like a slavish worker bee serving its queen, I worked mindlessly for so long that it never dawned on me what I had constructed. My career had blossomed into financial success, the money spent on building a prison, and the winds had turned against that house in hurricane force, threatening its destruction. Had I freed the bee with my dance or had the bee freed me with hers? I wondered, but either way, God moved us both out through the screen door and into the light of new air.

Standing on my back deck, a surge of satisfaction overcame me; an encouragement of spirit that I had not felt in many weeks. My heart leapt with joy and it was true happiness. This was all accomplished in secret for no one's notice. It was performed out of love, or responsibility, or gratitude, or madness, who knew and this time I would not analyze it, just accept it. My random act of kindness, so small and insignificant, unnoticed by anyone, had liberated my spirit along with my innocent captive. Our brief encounter revealed to me that goodness has no lower boundary. Even the smallest ray of light diffused a cathedral of darkness, and my dance with the honey bee was my first small ray of light that would wash the darkness out of my life in the coming months. How majestic to find the miraculous in something so small and an act so seemingly inconsequential. This indescribable world revealed the majesty of its design from the simplest thing to the most complex, from the visible to the invisible, from the finite to the endless, from the alone to the gathered, and from the imprisoned man to the freed bee. *"Kenny, be free!"*

Ÿ

Pam's garden, Ashland City, Tennessee

Chapter 5

« WALKING MAN »

"Moving in silent desperation, keeping an eye on the Holy Land, a hypothetical destination, say, who is this walking man?" (James Taylor, June 1, 1974)

The year pushed forward into the early summer months, where days grew longer and warmer, and at night, the sky stretched across the earth's arch like a twinkling blanket. I felt a stirring of returning optimism and reclaimed some emotional footing. I reached out to friends more often than I had in months, and also more frequently engaged my two sisters and children in correspondence. These were small acts on my part, but marked emotional improvements. Pam and I spent a lot of time talking, in many ways getting to know each other in a new light. I was working again, admittedly only part time, but the work helped me to regain a sense of purpose and responsibility. The opportunity required me to sell my skill set at a pay rate far below my historical grade, but I had no regrets. In the absence of work for those months prior, I realized that work fulfilled more inside of me than compensation. I needed both, but would take them as they came: *"To want what I have and take what I'm given, with grace,"* as encouraged by the beautiful words of Larry John McNally in one of my favorite Don Henley songs.

Since my fortuitous encounter with the bee, the winds turned in a more favorable direction. Every minute of every day I longed for things to be better. Although I really did not understand what specific actions that change would entail, I relied upon the notion that small acts of kindness would pay large dividends in my life. There were brief interludes of spontaneous joy and laughter. Pam was changing, too. It was reflected in her smile and eyes. She re-embraced her spiritual life which was so vitally important to her daily walk. Her steadfast, earnest prayers encouraged us through her unpretentious faith. The confines of our home, into which I had retreated, now smothered me, although we had made material strides in improving its livability. Just sitting around felt claustrophobic and I knew that I needed to get out of the house regularly and start moving around inside of life again. My part-time job took me into Nashville a couple of days a week, but on other days, when I had no work-related reason to leave our home, I could not stay there without feeling like a wild animal in a barred cage. On one of those days, I grabbed my keys, jumped into my truck, and headed to the greenway near our home with no particular intention other than to be moving. If nothing else, I could take a good walk.

At the time, we were living northwest of Nashville along the Cumberland River. Our small town of Ashland City had in the past years taken an abandoned stretch of railroad line and turned the four-mile pathway into a greenway that hugged the twisting Cumberland River bottomland. Inside the dense canopy of trees that covered the path, I walked alone, accompanied only by the whistling of the wind sweeping through the trees and the occasional distant horn of a tugboat making its way up the Cumberland River toward the Ohio River. It was glorious. The next day, I returned to walk again. As often as I could, I would go there to walk, think, pray, and hope. Moving was living.

In the early mornings before the sun would heat up the land, the plants and trees scattered across the dense canopy eased themselves into the new day, reaching with outstretched arms to capture the life-giving rays that streaked through the gaps in the treetops, forming thin pencils of light that fell to the ground like laser beams from heaven. On many days, I was the only person there to see the unveiling. Along the pathway, small animals foraged in the woods, going about their morning duties without allowing me to become a distraction. Early mornings were my favorite time to walk, when the air was moist and cool, and the river fog floated into the tree bank and seemed to muffle the noise of the world. I was almost always alone there, but I never felt lonely.

Among the few people that I would see with any degree of regularity was a tall, thin man, adorned in baggy gray sweats and a matching gray sweatshirt. He walked alone. Time after time, the solemn walking man and I greeted one another on the greenway, exchanged short but pleasant acknowledgments, and passed on by one another like two ships in the night. There was something about the walking man's disposition that led my senses to believe that troubles were at his door, and that he was struggling through a great trauma. Given his frequency on the greenway, I assumed that he was out of work as well, but his deep set eyes revealed something weightier, more profound and deeply entrenched in his psyche. I felt his loss in my spirit as we passed one another, like a gravitational tug against my soul's orbit, but I dared not the courage to speak with him beyond our casual greeting for fear of intrusion.

I talked frequently during this time with my friend, David Mathews, who was a grief counselor and Church of Christ minister in Searcy, Arkansas. David had dedicated the last several years of his life working with hurting people at their retreat center in Texas. He and his wife Debbie named the organization, *Spark of Life*. It was a beautiful metaphor for the process of healing that they had found in their own lives after the death of a grandchild. They taught that people often required twelve to fifteen months of recovery time from a traumatic event. I wondered how far along that path of healing the walking man had borne his consignment of suffering. His fixed gaze revealed to me a man living deeply inside of himself. I rarely caught his eyes for more than a brief second during all of our exchanges, but in the few instances where our eyes did meet, I recognized the hollow darkness that emptied into the soul of a man in the midst of great anguish. As time went on during the summer, Pam often joined me on the greenway, along with our two Dachshunds. As we encountered the walking man, we often speculated between ourselves about the details of his circumstances. Neither of us had any desire to impose ourselves upon him, but as fellow sojourners in the battle of life, we were willing to assist him within our capabilities. There was a compelling pull for us to know more, not to satisfy our curiosity, but somehow we felt that there was a common story that perhaps, if shared, would offer him comfort. The opportunity to engage him did not come that summer, so the circumstances of his life were left for us not yet to know, but he kept walking.

My work that summer remained steady but not full-time, which would have been an awful burden to bear under normal circumstances. As fate arranged it, the part-time work afforded me more time on my hands than I had experienced for a decade. It was time that I needed and savored, so I walked and walked for hours on end and thoroughly enjoyed the relief of daily responsibility. I was reacquainting myself to my God and I found Him no matter where I went, as my frequent excursions had now extended beyond the opportunities afforded me locally. Failure had surprisingly delivered me the luxury of contemplation. Failing in the eyes of the world was not the ending blow that I always feared and the healing process held its own surprises as well. From some angles, I was beginning to see it as a blessing, although embracing this notion at the time was too difficult, too near, and too early. Failing allowed me to start over. I wasn't just healing – I was reinventing myself, and *reinvisioning* the new man I hoped to become. As to my vocation, I pursued every opportunity that came my way, and initiated many others, but I had learned that the outcomes were not my responsibility. Although uncomfortable, it was like my father always told me, *"From the bottom, there's only one way to go, and that's up!"*

Soon I found myself extending my walking territory, and one of the first new places chosen was Montgomery Bell State Park, near White Bluff, Tennessee, in Dickson County. This was familiar ground for me and close to our old home. Pam had worked at the park as a lifeguard during high school. It was here that she rescued a drowning swimmer one summer, perhaps saving the young man's life. During that same summer, Kurt wiggled himself into park employment on the maintenance crew, doing odd jobs which principally included riding around in the park's pickup truck looking at the female campers. The state park had twenty-five miles of walking paths and winding trails that crisscrossed three beautiful lakes hemmed in between its pine and oak tree-lined hollows. Over the remaining summer months, and into the early fall of the year, I walked every trail that the park had to offer, and many of them I walked dozens of times, cheerfully following the small brooks and winding streams from their sources to the pooling lakes below. One of the more remote spots on the main Montgomery Bell Trail was a log dugout named Hall Shelter, where I often rested and meditated. The old hut held a secret, though. If you took the time to note the small trail leading down the hill from the shelter, you would find a brier thicket at its end, and after that, the trickle of a pristine brook. Just uphill from the brook, a natural spring oozed pure, cool water from hidden places inside the earth and collected in a small holding pond that served as the head waters for Hall Creek.

Hall Shelter on the Montgomery Bell Trail, Dickson County, Tennessee

On warmer days, I frequently enjoyed a clasped handful of the liquid refreshment and often splashed the cool water across my face with equal pleasure. Other times, I would simply stare with religious devotion at this reflective marvel of creation. I felt healing powers at work here, and on mornings when the warmth of the day drew the mist from the cool waters, fairy-like patterns danced along the surface of the small pond to a song and rhythm known only to God. I only witnessed the fairy mist dance a few times, but I can attest that they occurred. The natural pace of the woods and the sounds of water filled me with new energy. I was a thief to awareness and insight for far too long, but this time alone in the woods heightened my senses to fresh horizons. It took time to seek out the simple and the small. I listened. When I wanted to walk, I walked. When I wanted to pause, I paused. In and among the trails of the forest, time and solitude were my kind companions. I began to wonder at what price I would trade to have everything as it was before, denying the truth of how badly it was broken. It was so much better to know, and live inside of the pain of the knowing, than not to know and have the pain hidden from me. The truth drew me to God like a moth to a candle. My crushing was not punishment – it was salvation.

In the early fall of that year, on one particular morning while driving to walk at Montgomery Bell, my mind shifted instead toward thoughts of the Narrows and the sounds of rushing water. The water was high upon my arrival at the park's parking lot, partially covering the wooden steps that led to the river's edge at the kayak launch. Incoming rain looked more certain than probable at this point, so I decided instead of walking the high ridge trail that I would redirect to the shorter side trail which led to the tunnel's outlet side. It took no more than a ten minute walk until I stood before what most engineering historians believed to be the oldest tunnel in America. Throngs of water rushed forth from the hole carved into the side of the mountain. Honed by the sweat and blood of forced slave labor, it was now something to honor and cherish. As nature used fire to forge itself into beauty, and thorns scattered among the roses, such was the case in the birth of this beautiful land. Civilization had wiped out the aboriginal peoples that built the ancient mounds a thousand years ago in my view just across the river. Slavery had brutalized humans, compelling their labor and skills solely for the benefit of their masters. The man whose face and brief history was shown on the park pavilion display next to me came to this country not because of its beauty, nor to render kind service to its inhabitants, but rather, to strip it with raw ambition and brutality, as Montgomery Bell, the namesake of the nearby park and this historical tunnel, settled into this part of the Tennessee plateau in 1802. The ambitious industrialist was summoned by the iron-rich dirt, cheap land, slave labor, and virgin timber needed for the charcoal which fueled the intense flames of the iron furnaces he constructed throughout the region. The land and its bounty turned Montgomery Bell into one of the country's largest suppliers of pig iron bar. The dirt could give life or have life taken from it. Bell was a taker. It was here that he exploited the dirt and built his fortune, and here that he met his end, dying alone. His once admirable home is now completely dilapidated, an unrecognizable pile of rubble in the woods nearby, his furnaces sold or abandoned, and no heirs to honor his name forward. The grand Pattison Forge which stood adjacent to the outflow hole of the tunnel was long gone, having been constructed by Bell and his partner, Joseph Hardin. Hardin's interest in Pattison Forge was sold upon his mother's death near Nashville and his subsequent return to Arkansas, where he rejoined his brother Joab at the Cadron Settlement. Before his death, Bell tried to rescue his miserable life by repatriating some of his slaves to Liberia, but only after they had made his fortune secure. It was left for God to discern the truth of Bell's remorse, if any, but his legacy forged from cruelty was what we continued to honor, inexplicably.

I squatted down on a nearby stone along the gravel pile that lined the river's edge and stared at how much rock was hand-honed from this bluff. I envisioned dozens of strong, dark men crammed into the tight cavern with picks, shovels and buckets, their names known now only to God. I considered the grotesque nature of our whitewashing of southern history, whereby we attributed honorarium of their forced labor upon the very individual that bought and sold those men like cattle. *"Bell's Tunnel,"* was a tunnel of oppression, yet through his name we continue as a people to promote the perpetrator of this brutality rather than acknowledge his victims. Only a simple reference existed on the park's display, as almost an afterthought, which read, *"...the arduous labor was done by slaves."* It seemed more appropriate that this tunnel should be stripped of its name, of any

"Bell's tunnel was almost certainly constructed using the long established method known as hand drilling, which utilized hand-held hammers, chisels, and black powder; the arduous labor was done by slaves." (National Historic Landmark description #71000814)

name, and be left as nameless as the men who chiseled through the mountain bedrock. I had made many trips to this place over the years, but only on this morning was the weight of oppression revealed to me so clearly, so palpably. The weight of sin was deceivingly light in its provisioning and exhaustingly heavy in its rendering.

Returning home, still soaked from the rain that met me along the short path back to the parking lot, I found Pam sitting on our back porch wrapped in a throw and looking out at the river in the distance toward the bridge. She was off on that day and looked upset about something, hardly noticing that my clothes were still wet. I asked her what was wrong. She told me that earlier that morning she decided to take the pups for a walk at the small city park near the boat ramp by the Ashland City Bridge. It was there that she soon came upon the walking man. As was always the case, he was dressed in his gray sweat pants and floppy gray Hoodie. She said that something inside of her moved her to speak that morning, and not just as a passing greeting, but to speak where the man would have no exception but to respond to her attentiveness with a return conversation. Her assertiveness was effective. The walking man's name was Randall, and he was married with children, who were all reared in Cheatham County. He acknowledged seeing us often and recognizing our two Dachshunds. Pam told Randall that we often spoke of him, and we wondered if he was struggling with some great trauma whereby we could assist or share in his grief. She spoke briefly of our desert experience; the hard time that we were still going through, and the many unresolved issues that contributed to it and had been exposed as a consequence.

Standing in the morning fog that was rolling off of the river, Randall began to pour out his emotional story to Pam as if they were the oldest and closest of friends. He related that for years he worked in Nashville for a large construction company, until losing his job in a sudden sale of the business. Prior to that loss, he had never been without work since high school, and the emotional strain from that event sent him into a mental tail spin from which he was struggling to recover. His mental agony began to affect his physical health over a year earlier, and as one fell, the other fell farther, and the cycle of repetition was fixed. It was a pattern that Pam had witnessed far too closely in my life. At the time of his termination, Randall was a man of normal height and weight and reasonably balanced lifestyle. Feeling like he would go crazy sitting at home all day, he started walking in order to relieve some of the stress accumulating around his situation. *"It was the last thing that I still had control over,"* he told her.

His walking, which had begun as a blessing to him, became an obsession over a brief period of time. He began having guilty feelings about not walking long enough or far enough. Without work as a distraction, walking soon became what defined him and completed him. Not walking was failing, again. The demons, of course, tortured his mind when at home, but in the open air he seemed escape their grasps. As his walking obsession increased, an eating disorder followed, and the days and weeks turned into months, and then spread across two or three years, at which time Randall had almost completely stopped eating and walked constantly. Losing nearly eighty pounds, therapists and counselors were of no use to Randall, and his loving family watched helplessly as he melted away to literal skin and bones. The disease had almost ruined every relationship of those who loved him, and was now so pervasive, as he related to Pam, *"I'm probably not going to be able to fix this before it finishes me."*

Pam was at a complete loss as to how to respond to the tortured walking man, but offered him her sincere daily prayers for his healing. She cried in his presence over his woefully tragic tale, and they parted company. Randall walked away in his familiar gait toward his uncertain fate. For most of the day, Pam told me that she had been pondering Randall's life and could find no reconciliation within her own spirit. Had a demon captured Randall or had his mind created a demon captor? Either tragic answer to the question was exacting his will to live.

From time to time during the late summer, we continued to see Randall at the greenway or down by the park near the boat ramp, at which opportunities we engaged a brief conversation, always asking about his health, making small talk about the dogs and the weather. At the conclusion of every conversation, a burden filled our spirit, but with hope that the man would somehow, in God's grace, find a way out of the bleakness of his mind. Pam's work moved to full-time in early September, and my routine travels began to take me out of town to Asheville, North Carolina, our new adventure. We soon lost touch with Randall and never knew his last name. Since then, the image of Randall sometimes frequents my mind, especially at times when I recall our struggles in Ashland City, and the days of my own wanderings. I could still see the tall, thin man with the slumping gait, and the baggy gym clothes, and recall his story of how all seemed lost. Where only a small spark of life remained, a man was so lost inside the recesses of his own mind that he became ambivalent toward the miracle of life itself.

Through my wife's caring spirit and kindness, I witnessed what love can look like even on a foggy morning and to a desperate life, and I began to see something else: the miracle that was my wife, Pam. From within her brokenness, the heart of a lioness had emerged. During the worst of it, I was consumed with where to place fault, something or someone to blame, always measuring, promoting a certain justification, hashing through ancient history, but she was consumed only with loving her Lord and drawing deeper into His comfort. Pam retreated into grace, the safe place afforded her by her Keeper until the sorting out was completed. She hurt for people in pain, like Randall, in her soul, into the fiber of her being, while I hurt for the grief-stricken mostly in my mind, empathetic but still from a safe emotional distance. I could not reach the depths of my wife's natural sympathy. Her tears were tears from God's own heart, revealing a kinship of suffering that I could only watch and admire from a distance. Somewhere along my road toward ambition, I lost my place as her worthy champion and it hurt to know it. I had cast her out as much as she had run from me, but Pam was returning to me now, gentle portion by gentle portion, as the man that she had once loved, and then watched as love faded, stood ready to greet her back with open arms and a broken heart. Watching her speak of her encounter with the walking man, she transformed into the angel that I first fell in love with thirty years ago. All I could think about was how much I adored her and how afraid I was that she love me that much in return.

Pulpit Rock, Narrows of the Harpeth

Chapter 6

« CHAPEL »

In anticipation of college football and colorful athletic splendor, the approaching autumn greatly lifted my countenance. A new venture, Exsol Labs, was slowly becoming more viable as a business and demanded more of my time in Asheville. My two partners and I settled upon an arrangement with a steady income and health benefits, and it was a welcomed deal. Soon thereafter I began traveling to western North Carolina on a weekly basis. While the trip was long, it was also beautiful, so much so that I was rarely burdened by the five-hour journey; however, a hotel room was not a home, and on the weekends I looked forward to getting back to my family and the routine responsibilities of being a father and husband. I still took time to walk along my favorite paths at Montgomery Bell, the Narrows on rarer occasions, and the greenway along the Cumberland near our home. Things started to feel more like normal, like they had before, but better. There was less tiptoeing around topics of discussion, and we had a little money for entertainment. Aaron was in San Diego and actually loved it, although he still hated the Navy. The love affair I built with the woods during my rebuilding remained, and I was in search of its embrace on the morning I returned to the trails of Montgomery Bell State Park in late September to retrace one of my favorite walks that began at the back of the park property near Hall Cemetery.

While in Asheville the week before, I visited a favorite browsing location for books located among the eclectic shops of its downtown. Drifting around Malaprop's Bookstore and Café, I noticed a paperback copy of *The Life of the Bee* by Maurice Maeterlinck, an ancient book written about the author's observations as a lifelong beekeeper. The book looked slightly tattered and its pale green cover was faded with age, yet given that it was 100 years old, it was still in great shape. I walked to the checkout counter with the book in hand where a young woman of about twenty, wearing a tie-dye bandana and plastic beads around her neck, checked me out. My "*dance with the bee*" (as I had come to reference the event in my own mind) was taking on a religious significance through my reflection of our brief interlude earlier that spring. In my bones, I knew that a lesson from God had been shown to me on that day. Since then, I could see that irrespective of the size or complexity of anything in this creation, its design was skillfully and intricately woven, and it had value. There was nothing created that did not have value.

The book traveled with me on my return trip to Nashville. I brought it with me that morning to the park, fully intending to find a nice spot and take some time among its pages. I parked my truck just off the cemetery circle drive at the back of the park where it was convenient to pick up the Montgomery Bell Trail. I altered my normal path through the woods, breaking trail, and made my way down to a remote corner of Woodhaven Lake that afforded me a picturesque view of the lake and the spillway at its far end. Here I found the nice sunny plot of ground that I hoped to find. A slight breeze pushed its way across the clear lake, causing small waves to lap over the shoreline with an occasional splash. I noticed two men fishing from a johnboat in the shallow water near the mouth of the creek. They did not look that busy with fish. Other than their presence, I was alone. I rooted out a grass nest and began thumbing through the yellowed pages containing Maeterlinck's words.

Through a lifetime study of bee behaviors and their hardwired instincts, Maeterlinck concluded profound truths about nature and mankind. Among the pages dedicated to the bees, the author shared his direct and intimate experience in very personal language that revealed an emotional attachment far beyond only scientific interests. Discovering that another soul had fallen in love with the fickle bee only added to the enchantment of my "*dance with the bee*" experience. She was, in truth, such a sexy creature, indeed! The chapter entitled *The Nuptial Flight* caught my eye, and I flipped to it, settling into a peaceful reflective posture so as to take in the wisdom of the century old pages. Maeterlinck related how he loved the creatures so completely that he struggled emotionally and intellectually with the reality of their brutality. Within the context of all of their other functions, the bees conformed to a life of working only for the social good, a sacrificial life of total servitude; however, when the time came to change the queen in order to fulfill that ordained continuance of the hive, the horrors of the true costs of the commitment bore such poor resemblance to the docile creatures that he loved, that he wrestled within himself for arguments to avoid the truth of their actions. It was their polar dual nature that so disturbed his sensibilities: one nature, giving and cooperative, co-existed with another nature which was callous, calculated and brutal. As Maeterlinck pondered these notions, he recalled a conversation that he had with an old friend, "*a great physiologist,*" who related the following story on a long walk they took together across the English countryside of Suffolk, the same landscape that inspired W. G. Sebald to write *The Rings of Saturn*.

"This is no truth for us yet, but there are everywhere three semblances of truth. Each man makes his own choice, or rather, perhaps, has it thrust upon him; and this choice, whether it be thrust upon him, or whether, as is often the case, he have made it without due reflection, this choice, to which he clings, will determine the form and the conduct of all that enters within him.

The friend whom we meet, the woman who approaches and smiles, the love that unlocks our heart, the death or sorrow that seals it, the September sky above us, this superb and delightful garden, wherein we see bowers of greenery resting on gilded statues, and the flocks grazing yonder, with their shepherd asleep, and the last houses of the village, and the sea between the trees, -- all these are raised or degraded before they enter within us, are adorned or despoiled, in accordance with the little signal this choice of ours makes to them. We must learn to select from among these semblances of truth. I have spent my own life in eager search for the smaller truths, the physical causes; and now, at the end of my days, I begin to cherish, not what would lead me from these, but what would precede them, and, above all, what would somewhat surpass them."

The two men continued advancing up to a hilltop overlooking a beautiful valley below, where some peasant people were working to take up their corn. The physiologist friend noted to Maeterlinck that from their distance and perspective, one could only see the beauty of the work being performed, as the people went silently about the very human tasks of tending their fields and collecting the food that would store them through the winter. The two men agreed, as they stood watching the villagers perform their daily labors, that there was nothing that could be added by man or nature that would make the scene more beautiful or more serene. From this vantage point, in the abstract of the ideal, their minds could not conceive a desecration of the beauty of the thing before them, and joy rose up inside of their spirits, with thoughts only of peace and splendor. As it was with the bees, so it was with ourselves; desiring the most noble of values but so often succumbing to the vilest of our natures, unable to draw from the Spirit the strength required to love completely. At the height of zeal, as the scene in all of its loveliness engulfed them, the physiologist friend noted further:

"I have studied these people for many years. We are in Normandy; the soil is rich and easily tilled. Around this stack of corn there is rather more comfort than one would usually associate with a scene of this kind. The result is that most of the men, and many of the

women, are alcoholic. Another poison also, which I need not name, corrodes the race. All of them, men and women, young and old, have the ordinary vices of the peasant. They are brutal, suspicious, grasping, and envious; hypocrites, liars, and slanderers; inclined to petty, illicit profits, mean interpretations, and coarse flattery of the stronger. Necessity brings them together, and compels them to help each other; but the secret wish of every individual is to harm his neighbor as soon as this can be done without danger to himself.

The one substantial pleasure of the village is procured by the sorrows of others. Should a great disaster befall one of them, it will long be the subject of secret, delighted comment among the rest. Do not imagine that the sight of this marvelous sky, of the sea which spreads out yonder behind the church and presents another, more sensitive sky, flowing over the earth like a great mirror of wisdom and consciousness – do not imagine that either sea or sky is capable of lifting their thoughts or widening their minds. Nothing has power to influence or move them save three or four circumscribed fears, that of hunger, of force, of opinion and law, and the terror of hell when they die."

I closed my book and pondered these words, straining through the dichotomy of the human condition as related in this telling. I reflected upon the villagers in the story, and how good and bad existed within them at the same time. The angle of the view changed the reality. As they wore their beauty, they wore their sins. Who they were and what you believed them to be depended upon your observation point and personal opinion. Was this not the circumstance of us all, struggling to be seen as good in the eyes of God? The victors always reserved the opportunity to write the history and determine the heroes and villains, more often than not through conquests of brutal force. They chose the angle of the viewing lens that history would gaze through. Over the course of my own brief lifetime, I rarely failed to see evil perpetrated without the blessing of a god who would fulfill the notions of warped idealism. The question begs, "Whose God?"

The bees bowed to forces of nature that were far beyond their capacity. The one thing that they lived to do was to survive long enough to allow the next generation to live. They had free will, also. They could fly far off into the ether, but they did not. The bee that was freed from my home could have flown away into a new world, but with certainty it returned quickly to the hive from where it originated, yielding to an instinctive fear of isolation which compelled her continued servitude. Was it the reality of the bees that they *did not* fly away or *could not* fly away? God seeded into the bees the core values of survival and propagation, the same desires that drove our extrinsic human existence. Only our developed minds had the power to overcome these base instincts. I wondered if I had any similar and unseen boundaries. In our search to understand and render human *goodness*, what was truly *good*, and for whom was it good for?

Leaving the sanctuary of my spot by the lake, I walked around the outside perimeter of the park, following the trail until it merged with McAdow Creek, where I took pause to listen to the creek bubbling over the stones. The words from the book continued to trouble me, as they were designed to do, and my thoughts wrestled with one another. Had I defined my *truth* through a perspective of my own observations? I wondered how much of life was played out already, built inextricably into the design, without my noticing that I had little to do with the vast majority of my individual outcomes. Like the bees, I looked free from a distance, but in reality, I was bound by invisible barriers that I did not see and could not understand. My free will was encapsulated within boundaries defined by my design, forced to contend with the propensities of my DNA, the depth of my experience, the harshness of my environment, and the demands of my faith. All these conditions worked in unison to frame me, to measure me, and to contain me. In this multiplex of human existence, would God grant me grace given imperfect actions emerging from pure intentions? I recalled the ancient words of

Meister Eckhart, who said, *"Truly, it is in the darkness that one finds the light."* Perhaps the darkness was telling us that without it, the light would offer no refuge.

I stepped up onto the small bridge that crossed McAdow Creek, and leaned against its log rails as I saw my own reflection in the pool below. Looking down at my worn, wrinkled face, I knew that I had in the past exchanged the ache of truth for the comfort of lies, hoping for outcomes of life that were never promised to me. I projected goodness where it did not exist and rendered evil upon innocents, all in the name of making myself comfortable with my own choices: making myself belong. Even in this placid ground, the beauty of man and his wretchedness walked side by side across the decades of time. Many sins were allowed to shame my life which, now in reflection, may not have been sins at all, but of living a life within the boundaries of values instilled by faith and my own personal decisions about how to survive in a brutally competitive world. What man would receive the most grace – the good man that did a bad thing or the bad man that did a good thing – was either man different than the other? These were great and confounding mysteries, and my thoughts were incapable of resolving them. The true sins seemed always easier to recognize when looking back upon them in the light of their consequences than when living through them. True sins result in consequences that last.

The dichotomy of our life in God is defined by its duality. No more than a few hundred yards from the exact place where I stood, was an iron forge owned by ironmaster Richard C. Napier, a contemporary of Montgomery Bell. Laurel Furnace, located on Jones Creek, like Pattison Forge along the Harpeth River, produced pig iron as a supply input to the Turnbull Forge located a few miles away. At Laurel Furnace's high point around 1820, it boasted a workforce of nearly one hundred persons, almost all of whom were slaves. The quality of its iron by all accounts was without equal across the South. Around this same time, an itinerant Presbyterian preacher named Samuel McAdow moved to the area from Kentucky and established a homestead. The water beneath my feet was his life giving stream. McAdow was said to be a man *"of melancholy temperament,"* who was also hard-working, trustworthy, and wholly dedicated to the Gospel of Christ. He was raised and began his preaching career, near Guilford County, North Carolina, before migrating west along with many Scotch-Irish families looking to improve their lot in life. After the death of his first wife, he moved to western Kentucky, and then later south to Dickson County, Tennessee, where he and two other pastors separated from the Presbyterian Church and established a new denomination, the Cumberland Presbyterian Church. The new Christian denomination was chartered in 1810 within the sound of the hammer strikes and slave songs of the laborers of Laurel Furnace.

From its inception, the main goal of the Cumberland Presbyterians was to meet the expansion efforts of rival denominations in the pioneer settlements of the western territories. Given that few ordained and educated men were excited at the prospects of living in the wilds of Indian Territory with their families, the Cumberland Presbyterian Church filled many of its outlying pastor quotas with willing lay ministers. Layman pastor John Carnahan received one of the church's first assignments to bring the Word to the heathen settlements of the Arkansas territory. He settled at Crystal Hill, a community located between Little Rock and Cadron, and preached to crowds from Poke Bayou to Cane Hill. A sandstone chapel was constructed on park grounds to commemorate the founders of the denomination and their westward expansion of the gospel. The three honored men are Samuel McAdow, Samuel King, and Finis Ewing, a wealthy Kentucky slaveholder and later noted instigator against the Mormon expulsions from Jackson County Missouri.

"The first evil I shall mention is a traffic in human flesh and human souls. I fear, some of my Cumberland brethren do not scruple to sell for life their fellow-beings, some of whom are brethren in the Lord. And what is worse, they are not scrupulous

to whom they sell, provided they can obtain a better price. Sometimes husbands and wives, parents and children, are thus separated, and I doubt not their cries reach the ears of the Lord of Sabbath. Indeed, they seem by their conduct toward them, not to consider them fellow-beings." (Finis Ewing, Cumberland Presbyterian Church)

The chapel held a place of admiration in my heart more than its honorary history. Stains of my tears dotted the rock floor and echoes of my cries swirled among its wooden rafters. God and I wrestled here with one another in an openness and intimacy that was hard for me to find anywhere else on earth. I cried out all of my anguish and exposed all of my vulnerabilities while sitting alone on its heavy oak pews. When my spirit was inconsolable, only this place gave me renewal. I honored no other sanctuary built with human hands greater than this small chapel. It was a refuge for me in times of complete desperation.

The shrine area at the park also held another beloved memory. In the pool below my feet, a small crowd of parishioners stood beside the creek and watched Pastor Paul Tucker baptize my oldest daughter, Amber, in 1994. After meeting Paul, we decided to break with the standing family position of attending First Baptist Church and moved our hearts and hands to Dickson Cumberland Presbyterian Church. Paul Tucker and I met for the first time during Thanksgiving week of 1993. We were instant buddies. I was immediately taken by this young and enthusiastic pastor with his gregarious personality and infectious smile. Paul's pastorate, Dickson Cumberland Presbyterian Church, was founded upon the arrival of Samuel McAdow, and the congregation took great pride in its recognition throughout the denomination as being the home church associated with one of its founders, including responsibility for upkeep of the CPC shrine.

It was the first time in many years that my church life became significant and fulfilling. Being a part of DCPC was a joy for my entire family. We felt in lockstep with the community and its people. In addition to our love of the congregation, Paul and I soon became inseparable friends. In time, I began substitute teaching the primary adult Sunday school class, which I considered an honor. After some of our friends left the church to return to First Baptist, I took over the class full-time. My preparation for the weekly Bible study enforced a discipline for me to spend time in the Word, increasing my spiritual growth and optimism in my faith. Like the two men standing on the hill from the Maeterlinck story, watching the corn being taken into the barn, I could not imagine a greater church happiness than the happiness that we seemed to have found there. I was seeing it all then only from a distance.

Nearing the end of the second summer at the church, I received a call from Pastor Paul asking if he could stop by the house and talk with me. After some introductory remarks, he asked if I would consider serving as an Elder in the congregation. *"We need some new blood,"* he said, parting a grin across his face, *"and you're it."* Paul personally nominated me for this responsibility, but my confirmation would have to come from the Elders of the church. There were many decisions in my life that I made with little reflection or consideration, but this was not one of them. I did not jump in feet first. I searched my heart to know that I was ready for this responsibility, and with all of my hope I accepted the nomination a few days later. Paul was thrilled, and now it was up to the Elders to confirm me.

Everyone in the church knew that my appointment as an Elder would lend support for Paul's new ideas and efforts toward change. Many welcomed the fresh approach and enthusiasm that the young pastor brought to the older body of believers, substantially stooped in doing things the same way they had for decades. Others were not as quick to embrace change. As word of some opposition to my nomination began to filter into Paul's ear, he wanted to make me aware of the same, and called me, noting that he believed it to be mostly church gossip. I decided to wait and see what the Elder Board would have to say about my nomination, and after that vote, Paul and I agreed to reconsider my nomination if strong support for me was not evident with the Elders. Our concerns soon dissipated when my nomination a few weeks thereafter received unanimous approval from the current Elder Board at its monthly meeting and Paul was proud when he notified me of their vote. He took me to Houston's in Nashville where we rejoiced over a ribeye steak and baked potato at his expense. It looked like God was ready to do a great work in my life and that our young pastor had the leadership of the entire church behind him.

The final confirmation of committing a man to the work of the Cumberland Presbyterian Church as an Elder required a vote of its local congregation. In almost every case recalled by Paul and others, upon approval by the current Elder board, the individuals that comprised the congregation would follow suit. On the Sunday evening of my confirmation, to my surprise upon arrival at the church, something seemed amiss. I sensed a distance between others in the church and me, a distance that had not existed previously. I did not see Paul until the service began, and his eyes did not search me out as they often did. I knew in my soul that something was wrong. Pam and the children sat next to me unaware of my concerns.

The main order of business at the evening service was the appointment of the new Elders and events proceeded right to order. Two other men were also nominated to fill the three open positions. Our Chief Elder moved to the podium and read aloud the names of the nominees, mine among them. A vote of acclamation from the church congregation was requested as each man's name was read. The first man's name was read – all in favor. The second man's name was read – all in favor. When my name was read, a man that I barely knew stood up in the back of the room and made a motion to replace my name with the name of another. I was confused and bewildered and sought Paul's eyes for an explanation. Instead of staring back at me in disbelief, I could clearly see a veil of sadness fall over him. His dark expression told me that what he had feared the most was about to take place. The air inside the church sanctuary became heavy and thick to my breathing. Pam squeezed my hand and searched my eyes for an explanation. People sitting near us murmured among themselves like jurors watching a murder trial. I could find no other eyes to meet mine except Paul's. I felt like a man alone in an airplane that was nose diving into the ground while the spectators waited to see the crash. The man who had accepted the nomination in my place sat motionless beside his wife in a pew near the front of the sanctuary. It was an ambush.

I wanted nothing more than to get up and run away, but my family was there, and making an impromptu exit with three children would have caused even a greater scene. Paul stood slowly and deliberately approached the podium. Clasping the wooden structure with his hands on both sides, he acknowledged the strengths of the newly nominated candidate, but stressed also the historical procedures of the church body to honor the wishes of its leadership, as the Elder Board had unanimously approved my nomination. His words were strained, as if he was preaching someone's funeral. Although heartfelt, listening to him speak sent me deeper into despair. At the moment the pastor turned to sit down, unmoved by his encouragement, another man seconded the first man's nomination for my replacement. Paul retrieved a handkerchief from beneath his black robe and wiped a line of tears from his face. The Chief Elder acknowledged the new nomination from the speaker's podium as my shame grew greater with each word. What had I done, I wondered, or what had I failed to do? It was all over in a matter of minutes. I felt totally betrayed by the people that I thought loved me. Now I was seeing the village close in.

After that evening, it became easy to find something else to do on Sundays. I started to fish a lot and found welcomed peace on the water. I sought God often at the Chapel. Pam kept the kids going to DCPC for a brief time, but even she was wilting under the weight of the lamentable episode. We had several telephone calls voicing their support for us and saying how wrong it all had been, but it did not help heal the wounds. Finally, we stopped attending completely. Paul and I still talked and met and enjoyed each other, as did our wives, Pam and Darla. By this time there was an open acknowledgment by the Tucker's that Dickson would not be their church home for very much longer. Almost a day to the year after baptizing my daughter in McAdow Creek, Paul Tucker left the leadership of Dickson Cumberland Presbyterian Church, brokenhearted.

As the years of this event dissolved into the history of my life, it served as the beginning of the unmasking of many self-deluding myths about church and what people did beneath its banner and in its name. Indeed, whose God and for what good? The confirmation of my transformation would come in many forms and at many instances across the coming years of my life. Instead of needing God in my mind, I needed Him in my life. I was weary of worshiping an idea, an image, a set of rules, and another man's opinion. The troubling experience at DCPC sparked my journey of faith into a freedom of not needing to settle for being taught what to think by someone who was also taught what to think by someone. I did not need to belong to believe. Subsequently, I abandoned the teachings of mass delusion and became a man much more at home standing outside the institutionalized church looking in than one standing on the inside looking out. It was a shoe that would never again fit. Maeterlinck's recollections and observations of bees seemed to reveal the ultimate truth of the matter. The church looked more beautiful from a distance than from close up, more pure by reference than experience. Despite the heartbreak, the occurrence liberated me to live and to love under a set of rules of my own interpretation, rather than folding mindlessly into the historical beliefs of others. Being denied what I thought was best was God's way of showing me that He knew what was better for me. It was a customized suit of spirituality. Ultimately, I came to understand that my faith could not be outsourced.

Ÿ

Ruskin Cave Community, circa early 1900's Dickson County

Chapter 7

« RUSKIN »

"Now faith was the assurance of things hoped for, the conviction of things not seen." (Hebrews 11:1, *Holy Bible*, New American Standard)

In the small enclave of Walnut Grove in Dickson County, Tennessee, two spring fed streams converge to form Yellow Creek, a meandering thread of water that flows northwest toward the Cumberland River. At about the halfway point of its journey, the creek ambles through a lush valley surrounded by limestone bluffs where caves were carved eons ago. Ruskin and Jewel caves remain the king and queen of caves in this area, but dozens of smaller caves were also known by the locals in the Yellow Creek community. The creek held special memories for multiple generations of my wife's family, the Scotts. For as long as anybody could remember, Pam's father, Gus, accompanied children and grandchildren, cousins, aunts, and uncles to the swimming hole located about a half mile up a dirt road across from Ruskin Cave. It would be a breach of family protocol to reveal the exact location of the swimming hole, but the spot was within ear-shot of the field in 1862 where the retreating confederate General Nathan Bedford Forrest, and his troop of marauders, passed by on their way to Charlotte, Tennessee to resupply themselves and their horses. The wily and brutal commander and his men were fleeing the surrender of Fort Donelson, near Camden, to Brigadier General Ulysses S. Grant. The creek wraps through a valley as pretty as any Rockwell painting, surrounded by a rough limestone terrain, the dark pockets of rock between fractures hinting at the numerous pathways hidden beneath the soil. The largest and most famous of the underground caverns was Ruskin Cave, a massive hole sliced through the bedrock large enough to put a football field inside. The cave's history predates the county, and its spectacular location adjacent to the fresh waters of Yellow Creek ensured that indigenous peoples were using the cave long before the early pioneers lined it off with survey coordinates and began selling the selected plats to one another. When the railroad bypassed Ruskin in the 1860s, it spelled the doom of the valley as a potential center of growing commerce, which worked out just fine for the Scott family and their subsequent years of creek side leisure.

The remoteness that defined the area for a century as a respite for town folk also kept it out of reach of normal travel patterns, so across the years the land changed hands and purpose very little, but always there seemed to be a new plan to bring Ruskin out from obscurity and into prominence. During my lifetime alone, Ruskin had been a second home for country singer David Allen Cole, a private recreation area, a research center, and a day camp. By far, the most national notoriety for Ruskin Cave occurred in the late 1800's, when Julius Augustus Wayland, a magazine publisher with a proclivity toward socialism, took note of the fertile land and sparse population of the area and set about to build his vision of a utopian socialist colony. After a few years of fighting over the magazine and bath soap sales, the families attached to the ideal community started suing one another in Dickson County courts over land disputes. Wayland also skipped away to the Midwest from his grand experiment, starting a new magazine, *Appeal to Reason*. In an appeal to his own reasoning, Wayland decided upon his arrival in Kansas to maintain all of the profits of the new publication for himself and his family. Experience was always a good teacher. Looking for ways to expand his readership, Wayland reached out to popular socialist authors across the country for contributing articles. It was through this effort that he became introduced to a young novelist, Upton Sinclair. In 1906, Wayland ran a series of Sinclair's work which received wide acclaim in the large cities of the east and eventually led to the publishing of his masterwork, *The Jungle*, vilifying the meatpacking industry for its exploitation of migrant wage and worker conditions. The public outrage spurred by the book directly impacted the passage of the Pure Food and Drug Act that same year, and in this indirect manner, Ruskin had contributed to one of the major social movements in our country's history. As socialism waned under the constant drumbeat of its evils by conservative zealots, Augustus Wayland drifted into obscurity. In the wake of the death of his wife a few years later, he killed himself from an extended depression.

Across the road from where I parked was the long disbanded Ruskin Settlement, and before that, the Edgewood Normal School, a teacher college established by W. T. Wade, a wandering Virginian educator. Wade drifted into the county after teaching for years in Kentucky and other parts of Tennessee. He met and became a partner with fellow educator T. B. Loggins, and the pair assumed management of the Edgewood School in 1885, during a time when Ruskin was as heavily populated in its history as a settlement. Dreams at the time of growth and prosperity for the community proved fruitless when the railroad placed its terminus a few miles south in Dickson. The two administrators likewise soon moved the college closer to the rail line during the summer of 1891 and changed the name to Dickson Normal School. The school was very prosperous for many years at its new location and provided teaching curriculum to students from many parts of the state. Dickson Normal School graduated its most celebrated alumni in 1896, a young woman from the neighboring county of Humphreys, and the small Buffalo River town of Bakerville, Tennessee. Her name was Hattie Ophelia Wyatt. That same year, a young man from Carroll County, Tennessee named Thaddeus Caraway also graduated. Thaddeus and Hattie would eventually marry and move their family to Arkansas, where ten years later he finished law school and established a lucrative law practice in the northern part of the state. The Caraways settled permanently in Jonesboro and become one of the most highly recognized and regarded couples in the state's history. Hattie Caraway made history of her own, becoming the first woman elected to the United States Senate in 1932, succeeding her husband's earlier Senatorial service. Her former professor, W. T. Wade, lived out the remainder of his years in substantially less notoriety, remaining in the county of the school's namesake and joining with six other families in 1902 to form the Dickson First Baptist Church. The pastor of DFBC at the time of our marriage, Dr. Don McCoy, presided over our ceremony seventy-six years later in the home of Pam's uncle and aunt. Their statuesque two story home sat in the curve of the road leading to the location of historical Belleview Furnace, one of Montgomery Bell's iron forges, located along a stretch of Jones Creek near the old Rock Church, which Bell originally used as his headquarters before relocating them to Pattison Forge along the Harpeth River.

Breathing in the open air of Ruskin, I pondered our storied history with the largest church in the county. When Pam and I first married and moved to Dickson County, we immediately joined Dickson First Baptist Church where her family had been active members for half a century. We drifted away from and back into Dickson County, and First Baptist, on two occasions. Upon our second return, we decided to break from the family tradition and move our membership to Dickson Cumberland Presbyterian Church. We tired of the monotonous familiar pattern of following the family around, but the larger decision involved our evolving faith. Too many circumstances in life that deserved understanding and nuisance were presented at the Baptist church as clear distinctions, good or bad, black or white. I could not reconcile the complexities of the world through such a simple lens of analysis. My mind never worked well in conjunction with hard edges, and I hoped for a more reasonable doctrine from the Presbyterians. As a consequence we threw in with the young pastor, Paul Tucker, and his congregation.

We soon realized that the Presbyterians and the Baptists saw more things eye-to-eye than they differed, an experience which sealed the end of my affiliation with southern evangelicalism altogether. In our small town the selection of progressive faith viewpoints were nonexistent, and we were left without a home church. The safest harbor for Pam and the kids was back with her family at First Baptist. Mostly for the sake of my children, I agreed to submit myself to begging the Baptists to take me back, although I learned to view Sunday's like a necessary, but not enjoyable, visit to the doctor's office, something I had to do but couldn't wait until it was over.

During our time away, First Baptist called a new pastor in response to rapid growth in our bedroom community of Dickson. His name was Dr. John C. Compton, a determined and stoic man who accepted the senior pastor job at Dickson First Baptist with the goal of creating and funding a multi-million dollar building project. John had the perfect pedigree to lead a large Baptist congregation in the state of Tennessee. In John Compton, the church had a builder, a man of vision. We folded back into First Baptist with little fanfare and settled into a routine among familiar faces and names. After six months or so, we received word from Dr. Compton that he would appreciate a visit.

Upon his arrival, the conversation began friendly enough but quickly moved into my family's particular church and baptismal histories. Pam and I had been Baptist before, immersed in baptism, so we were all set with only a letter transfer. Our two youngest children had not yet made professions of faith, and in keeping with our faith tradition at the time, were not baptized as infants. With respect to Amber's baptism, I enthusiastically began to share with Dr. Compton the circumstances of Amber's beautiful baptism, a pouring, or affusion, that was intended as an immersion, for which McAdow Creek did not participate. I related how Pastor Tucker waded into the park creek with his dress trousers rolled up to his knees, about the water level being too low for an immersion, and how Amber had decided at that time, given the circumstances of the moment, to accept the traditional Presbyterian method of baptism. I told of how the family gathered together to pray for her, especially our happiness with the attendance and participation of her grandparents. We shared with him Amber's desire to be immersed to honor her grandfather's wishes and that desire was what led us to the outdoor venue in the first place, but we picked a bad day as far as water levels were concerned. We knew that Amber's baptism would not qualify her for Baptist membership, and that was fine. We had already spoken to her and she had already agreed to be re-baptized for a second time to meet the requirements of membership in the Baptist church.

During the entire time of my dialogue on Amber's background, Dr. Compton never smiled back. He sat unresponsive and listened, his thoughts drifting. At the instant of my conclusion, his brow furrowed, and he looked straight at me. *"Well, despite her intentions, Amber was not Biblically baptized by Pastor Tucker. She will certainly be required to be immersed, as you have already stated, and her baptism under immersion will fulfill God's commandment."* From the words drawn from his sentence, all I heard was his judgment, *"God was not pleased and did not accept her earlier baptism."* With respect to anything but immersion, the Presbyterians, Lutherans, Methodists, Moravians, Nazarenes, Congregational Christians, and Catholic churches, had it all wrong. All that was left for me to understand was that my beautiful daughter's perfect baptism at McAdow Creek was a sham that needed correcting.

As I considered the events and dialogue of that evening with Dr. Compton, it became clear to me that there were two types of people in the world: John Compton was one type, and I was the other. One of us saw the world in clearly distinguishable categories, either a *"this"* or a *"that,"* secured with the knowledge that it would always be that way, and therefore boldness should be utilized in promotion of that viewpoint. However you interpreted the angle, your interpretation was correct. I, on the other hand, saw things as always evolving, more complicated and nuanced as to *"good"* and *"bad."* Perspective and context were vital in my way of Biblical thinking, where I could not imagine that God did not completely desire that we mold our lives more into the values demonstrated in the Bible than we did its precepts. I saw perspective in the world where John Compton saw only holiness or sin. He saw black and white with clear distinctions, and I saw a great bridge that connected indistinct grays.

"I am a sect by myself, as far as I know." (Thomas Jefferson by letter to Ezra Stiles Ely, June 25, 1819)

My recollections returned to the present and I looked up into the bright sun to feel its warmth against my face. A flatbed farm truck turned into the road and slowly passed me, the wrinkled face of the farmer staring at me as if I were an alien, while a half-smoked cigarette bent from the corner of his mouth. I threw up my hand in acknowledgement of his curiosity. In some ways, to this place, this culture, I was an alien. I stooped down and picked up a small chunk of tilled dirt from the ground beneath my feet and crumbled it between my fingers, watching the wind blow the dust out of my hand. I could smell its musty earthiness. Pam and I started here, but we would finish somewhere else, and at our age, it was how we finished that mattered. I remembered tracing her beautiful form with my eyes on a hot summer day while she was lifeguarding at the Ruskin Camp pool so many years ago. She looked as beautiful today, to me, as then. The troubles that had come our way during the last couple of years were the blessing that we needed to wipe the slate clean and begin the time of our good ending. When W. T. Wade first rode into this immaculate valley and set his eyes across the landscape of Ruskin, how could he have imagined that a thread of his life would set in motion a vector of mine? But that's what happened.

Sometimes a bump is all that is needed to set one upon a different course. In life, one person chooses the well-worn path and the other chooses to search out an alternate route, each in hopes of finding their Shangri-La. After all, I had made the mistake in my past of confusing a person's depth of commitment with their knowledge and insight. Somehow it was too easy to infer special understanding onto individuals who most passionately argued the validity of their cause; however, so many times, these people were passionate, dedicated, convincing, and just wrong. It was not their passion that troubled me. It was my lethargy against it. Dogmatism required constant vigilance from the non-radicalized. Intolerance of something was always the enemy of the next step of forward progress. I wanted my life to be open to what God was trying to teach me now, not two thousand years ago.

And so it goes with God. (Piscine Patel, *The Life of Pi* by Yann Martel)

Chapel CPC Shrine
Montgomery Bell State Park

Chapter 8

« PAINT ROCK »

It was a rich and bountiful autumn. I remember it especially because of how the large maple tree near the back tree line of our home set against the blue sky, ablaze in color, like fueling a yellow torch. It stayed that way for several days until a cold front brought rain and stripped off many of the wilting leaves from its outstretched branches. I was feeling alive again. Without noticing it, I was drawn to my past, as if my spirit needed to revisit places that were not fully reconciled to my present life, the reemerged me. It was a perfectly timed occasion in mid-October that I received a call from my treasured friend, Professor Danny Powell. He encouraged me to join him at his cabin on Bull Shoals Lake for a weekend of *"the manly pursuits of crappie fishing, whiskey drinking, and guitar playing."* It was a long drive from Ashland City to northern Arkansas, but Pam encouraged me to go, and she could probably tell that I really wanted to. I arranged my North Carolina schedule with my business partner Rob and made plans to spend three days with Danny at his lake house located on the Missouri side of Bull Shoals Lake. On the prior Thursday morning, before daybreak, I packed my walnut Martin 000-18, tackle box, and several open-faced rods into my F-150 and headed west from Nashville on I-40. I intended to use the trip as a means of exploring several locations in the general direction of my journey to Bull Shoals. It was also a chance to go back and reconnect some of the dots of my youth.

By the time I passed through the southwest corner of Dickson County on the interstate, the breaking dawn burst through the rear window of my truck and began to warm the cab with its radiant glow. I set my destination on the historical river town of Smithland, Kentucky along a route that would take me across the Cumberland and Tennessee rivers and into Bluegrass Country, where the mighty Ohio and Tennessee rivers merged. The river town of Smithland acted as a launching spot for many fleeing slaves seeking help behind the Union lines by way of the Underground Railroad. It was also the place that my family, the Peels, fled the earthquakes and headed west into Arkansas. From there, I would work my way across the Ohio and Mississippi rivers at Cairo, Illinois, where two majestic steel girded bridges of impossibly narrow lanes still carried passengers on a chilling trip across those powerful rivers. My journey would mirror the path that my Peel pioneer ancestors followed as they moved from Smithland into the heart of the northern Arkansas hill country. As I neared the Tennessee River at Cuba Landing and stared across to the high bluff that demarcated the eastern-most portion of West Tennessee, I breathed in the fond memories of growing up in Jackson, and my youthful wanderings of the land squeezed between the Mississippi and Tennessee rivers.

In recent weeks, a mystical longing pursued me to reattach myself to those memories. On many nights during the summer and into the early fall, I looked at Google Maps for hours on end, studying the once familiar roads, tracing the paths of the rivers, and calling out the names of the townships and communities that defined my *"growing up in"* world. These places, and the people that comprised them, served as a catalyst to my early beliefs and ambitions, and although vast changes had occurred in how I viewed the world, I was compelled to tip my hat to their well-intentioned efforts. As the hum of the tires against the pavement kept a rhythm in my ears, and with my eyes set to the west, I believed that good days were coming.

At the last exit before the river, I turned north to follow Old State Highway 13, once a well-traveled stage coach route. The remote fertile valley that hugged the Duck River was majestic in its beauty and tranquility. A few farmhouses dotted the road, but they were easily outnumbered by the grain silos that served as witnesses to the abundance of seed crops grown across the bottomland. Near the junction point of the two rivers, the Buffalo and the Duck, the road bent through a heavily timbered area where rolling hills tumbled against one another, squeezing the feeder streams into narrow crevices that cut deep into the gaps between the hills. Expansive crop fields lined the Bakerville Road as it followed the twists and turns of the Buffalo along a decades old Chickasaw tribe hunting trail. Even with all subsequent improvements to the road since its creation, no one took the trouble to straighten out the crooked portions, as its path more resembled a ride at the county fair, hopping and dropping across the hilly countryside in unexpected directions.

The old town of Bakerville was all but abandoned years ago. Only a few families remained to knot the generations together and to hand down the family farm from old to young. Some generations embraced the farming lifestyle, while abandoned clapboard homes and dilapidated barns testified to the realities that most had given up the struggle and moved on to something different. Unlike the corporate farms that dominated southwestern Arkansas, individual family farms dotted the land in this valley. The ground was freshly tilled into perfectly spaced rows of mounded dirt, eager to heal during the winter from its spring and summer burden of nursing new seeds into maturity.

As I topped a small rise in the road entering the Bakerville community, I noticed a highly visible Historical Marker erected near the center of the crossroads. The silver and black plaque commemorated its most prestigious daughter, Hattie Wyatt, who grew up in this pristine rural village as the child of a grocer. Her family later moved a few miles downriver to Hustburg and eventually settled into the town of Johnsonville. Unlike most young girls of her time, young Hattie's family took pains to offer her a good education. At the age of seventeen, Hattie enrolled into Dickson Normal School, a teacher preparatory college located in the Ruskin community of Dickson County, a few miles east of Hustburg. It was there that Hattie met a young man from Carroll County, Tennessee named Thaddeus Caraway, whose older brother had paid for his advanced education by selling portrait tins around the communities of Huntingdon, McLemoresville, and McKenzie. The young students fell in love during the time of their college studies, both graduating in 1896 to accept various teaching jobs in and around the areas of their respective Tennessee home towns. After teaching for a few years, the ambitious Thaddeus moved to northern Arkansas to live with an uncle, where he studied to practice law. He was consequently admitted to the Arkansas Bar in 1900. Two years later, Hattie left Tennessee to join her new husband in the Ozark Mountains, where the couple made their permanent home at their edge in Jonesboro. From the beginning of his time in Jonesboro, Caraway quickly establish a lucrative law practice and became involved in the state's Democratic politics. A staunch advocate of President Woodrow Wilson, Thaddeus was expeditious in earning the reputation as a man dedicated to the working class white Arkansan and a defender of the American justice system.

He was a staunch segregationist. Caraway's precepts preceded him to the Legislative branch of the United States government from his days as a harsh District Attorney. While her husband was building his political career through the iron hand of widely acceptable prejudicial justice, Hattie Caraway spent her early married years making a home and raising three boys, as well as being active in Jonesboro, Arkansas's social scene. She would often accompany her husband on trips across the state to meet with constituents and attend local political functions, leaving the children in the care of the Caraway's full-time African American staff. One such trip took place in 1926, when the couple journeyed down Crowley's Ridge from Jonesboro to a small headwater swamp southeast of Brinkley, and participated in the dedication of a stone monument commemorating the location of the Initial Point survey for the Louisiana Purchase. It was on that date and place that Senator Caraway accepted conveyor deeds from the four grantors of the adjoining properties, the protected land henceforward to be managed under the guardianship of the government as an official Commemorative Monument of the United States of America. The Senator's wife sported a new bonnet purchased just for the occasion.

Reaching the end of Bakerville Road, I crossed the Duck River at Paint Rock. The view from the vantage point of the high bridge took my mind back to when I would come here to fish from the banks of the river. I pulled my truck around the sharp corner into the boat ramp area below the well-worn steel girded bridge that spanned the rock bluff from the levee. The old

Old Duck River Bridge – Paint Rock, TN

bridge was showing considerable signs of age as my eyes panned the rust and discoloration that had once been bright and clean and green. I wondered how much longer the gorgeous old structure would be able to hide from the wrecking ball of progress. As one of the few remaining pioneer roads that once lined the rivers, the Paint Rock Road remained a narrow, perilous national treasure. The bend in the road at the point where Paint Rock jutted out toward the Duck was so sharply constructed, and so poorly engineered, that modern vehicles could not move forward without exposing themselves to a blind spot on the other side. Locals in this area were obviously aware of this peculiar spot and moved far to the outside embankment of the road before attempting the blind turn to avoid scraping the paint off of the right side of their vehicle. Once the turn was accomplished, the road straightened along a high bank of the river that afforded a look back toward the bridge, and unveiled the emerald green waters of the Duck River that flowed southward over ancient boulders to the Tennessee. Monet would not have found a more perfect place to paint a breathtaking landscape. This small stretch of land, water, and sky always moved me, and I was again awestruck by its elegant and natural beauty. There was an odd, haunting power that I felt along these shores. The clouds hung heavy in the sky and hid most of the sun from view. Even on the brightest of days, the deep canyon always casts a foreboding gloom of beautiful, cool melancholy. As I watched the water move past me in rhythmic ease, I prayed that somehow things here would remain the same. People needed places that would not change. I scampered through the brush up the hillside and stood in the middle of the road and snapped a pic on my telephone, just as a ray of light broke through a swirl of purple clouds at the end of the steel structure.

Paint Rock was a rushing wind through my senses and a reminder of why I loved Tennessee so deeply, and it held more secrets than the Duck River crossing. History entertained no quarrel as to the arrival of stockman John Davis Howard to the Box Station area in the heavily treed hills between Hustburg and Paint Rock. Howard and his family moved here from southern Missouri during the summer of 1877. He and his wife, Zee, rented a large farm from the Banks Link family just downriver, and began to breed Dun horses that the budding horseman planned to race at the old Bloodhorse Race Track in Nashville. One of the horses from the Howard stall, Red Fox, developed a championship reputation in area racing circles, and Mr. Howard established an equally superb reputation as a country gentleman and as a responsible citizen among the residents of Humphreys County. Especially admired by the small community was the kind and charitable constitution of Mrs. Howard who seemed to never miss a chance to help someone in need.

Mr. Howard also had a close relative who lived north of Nashville in the White's Creek community. It was not an uncommon occurrence for B. J. Woodson to be in the area with John on days when the locals would gather for the horse races. The investment in raising race horses was understood by all involved to be a partnership between the two kinfolk, and the appearance of them together around Humphreys and Hickman counties was common and uneventful. Both men were particularly good shots, but especially J.D., who had demonstrated his skills for a broad audience at the local fair, impressing the bystanders with his uncanny shooting abilities and gun handling. By all accounts that remained to be told of the time spent in Humphreys County by the Howards and Woodson's, few men bore grievances toward either of them.

Original Railroad Levee, Old Johnsonville Road
Johnsonville State Historic Park

Born in Missouri, the son of a Baptist preacher and successful hemp farmer, J. D. Howard was an ardent Confederate and carried grudges against the North for what he considered to be the unwarranted invasion of the lives and property of white southerners. His parents were slave owners, and the boy became conditioned to the southern class structure and its economic dependency upon unpaid black labor. Despite his native state's duality on the topic of slavery, the young man enthusiastically signed on with the southern guerrilla Quantrill Raiders, whose atrocities against northern troops are widely documented by history. The Raiders gave the young man the outlet he needed to unleash his internal hatred upon the world, quickly forgetting the Biblical lessons from his slave-owner father, whose hollow words died in their own hypocrisy. A year after the arrival of the Howard family to Box Station, Mrs. Howard became pregnant, and eventually gave birth to two boys they named Gould and Montgomery, both of whom, only lived a few days. The small twins were buried on the edge of the Link farm. Marked only by two large creek stones, it was decades later before the nondescript headstones of the twin infant boys would be located. Upon verification of their identification as the infant sons of outlaw Jesse James, the bodies were reinterred at Mount Olivet Cemetery in Kearney, Missouri, near their father's boyhood home.

As the James Gang began again terrorizing the people in the Missouri territory, the established financial and political proponents of the state had reached their tolerance limit, fearing that the systemic news from James' raids throughout Missouri, as consistently reported throughout the eastern newspapers, would deter future capital investment in the region. In response to the pressure coming from government agencies and the railroad companies, Governor Thomas T. Crittenden issued a reward of $5,000 cash per man for the capture of Jesse or Frank James, dead or alive. The railroad companies shared the bounty expense with the state, and in an extraordinary act of governmental overreach, the state placed a death warrant upon one of its most infamous citizens without even a hint of concern for due process.

Commensurate with the assassination approval, the state took private money to finance the operation.

Governor Crittenden, and the railroad companies, employed Pinkerton guards to protect the train routes while numerous bounty hunters began searching for the notorious James brothers. Jesse James was soon killed by Robert Ford on April 3, 1882, shot in the back of the head, motivated by the posted reward and ensuing infamy. Fearing for his life after hearing of the death of his little brother, Frank James surrendered to Marshalls in Jefferson City, Missouri, on October 5th of that same year. Thomas T. Crittenden received wide praise for his commitment to eradicate the intolerable risk of interruption of commerce across his frontier state of Missouri, not to mention the lengths to which he demonstrated his willingness to use governmental power to murder a citizen, albeit a deprived one. The long run of terror from J. D. Howard and B. J. Woodson ended at the bequest of a different type of criminal enterprise, i.e., politicians performing the will of corporations. Deadly force, as a choice of political conflict resolution, had also resulted in the death of Henry W. Conway, the postmaster of Little Rock. It was twenty years earlier that politician Conway was killed in a duel at the hands of the Missouri governor's uncle, Robert Crittenden, the early Acting Territorial Governor of Arkansas, co-conspirator of land speculator William Russell, and founder of the Rose Law firm of Little Rock, where Hillary Clinton practiced as a young attorney. In the hands of an unrestrained government, what was illegal for citizens became legal for their elected representatives.

At Paint Rock, the Duck River bent from its northwestern tract and turned southwest toward the Tennessee River. The river widened appreciably after the bend into a broad area of swampland that stretched over the last four mile journey before blending into the northern flowing waters of the Tennessee. Heading west, I followed Old State Route No. 1 along the broad channel until the road dead-ended into the Tennessee River at the forgotten town of Hustburg, a once thriving community nestled into a peninsula framed by the Duck River on its south and the

Tennessee on its west and north. The only remnants of the original town were scattered clapboard homes and a couple of abandoned store buildings that stood with an air of pride indicative of long forgotten better days. The grand Tennessee River narrowed its channel at this location, which precipitated the success of the Trotter's Ferry that operated here long before the railroad bridge was completed downriver at New Johnsonville. The original structure built across the broad Tennessee River was the result of the work of The Nashville and Northwestern Railroad Company, chartered by the Tennessee State Legislature in 1852 to build a rail line connecting Nashville with Hickman, Kentucky for travel across the Mississippi River into Missouri and Arkansas.

Years later, as General Sherman's troops began their march to the sea, the railroad extension from the Tennessee River into Nashville ensured that supplies could reach the northern aggressors in a timely response to their track of carnage across the state of Georgia. The completed Union Army line ran from downtown Nashville, west through Kingston Springs, White Bluff, Dickson, Waverly, and then Johnsonville, where it terminated at the Tennessee River, the place where Nathan Bedford Forrest made a point to stop its further progress.

In the retrospect of history, Sherman did not need the supply line to conquer the south and thrust his way to the sea at Savannah. The extraordinary lengths that the Union Army engaged to build the railroad, and the desperate measures that the Confederates employed to destroy it, did not directly affect the outcome of the war. Just prior to the end of the Civil War, in 1864, at the completion of the rail line, President Abraham Lincoln appointed Military Governor Andrew Johnson over the lands of Tennessee which came under Union control. Johnson, in a brief ceremony on May 10th of that year, traveled the length of the completed rail line from Nashville to the river to make a speech commemorating the accomplishment, the labor of which had almost exclusively been at the hands and backs of African American soldiers and conscripted slave runaways. The pompous politician renamed the terminus city in his own name taking credit for an outcome for which he had made no contribution. It was unthinkable on that day of celebration that circumstances of the country would unfold so violently that within less than a year's time, Andrew Johnson, now the namesake of this shabby river town, would become the 17th President of the United States upon the assassination of Abraham Lincoln on April 15, 1865.

When the Corps of Engineers flooded the area in 1944 to make way for Kentucky Lake, the town of Johnsonville was forced to find higher ground. The town moved approximately four miles to the south, up river, and established the city of New Johnsonville, the site of one of the Tennessee Valley Authority's remaining coal powered, fossil fuel, electrical generation facilities, which burned through approximately twenty million pounds of coal per day, complements of the same rail line first conceived by the Union Army. Just east of the steam plant, I turned off of Highway 70 west toward Lucas Harbor, following the earthen embankment that held the original track of the Nashville and Northwestern Railroad line, this segment constructed in large

Library of Congress

part by the 12th, 13th, and 14th U. S. Colored Infantry. After its completion, the soldiers that built it were placed in charge of guarding the adjoining depots between Johnsonville and

Nashville. Their efforts targeted protecting the line from Confederate damage at the hands of sympathizers or renegades. The dirt covered, narrow road that led from the highway down to the boat dock ran the length of the two mile stretch as straight as a plum line, where pools of murky backwater overflowed from the bay on either side of the levee. The labor to build such a structure must have been enormous, but as with many accomplishments of historical noteworthiness, the credit of the endeavor went to the talkers rather than the doers.

African American volunteers and conscripted runaways formed the majority of Colored Infantry and Artillery troops. Later, they were assigned to garrison support and railroad protection of the Nashville-to-Johnsonville supply link. After observations of a direct charge against Confederate lines by the 13th Regiment at Overton Hill (Peach Orchard Hill) in the Battle of Nashville on December 16, 1864, the heroism of the noble men that served in these Colored Union regiments was noted in an official report by Confederate General James T. Holtzclaw. While sustaining heavy and consistent casualties, and without rear support, the men of the 13th Colored Regiment continued to charge the Confederate line, losing five standard-bearers in the attack. As one flag bearer would be killed, another soldier would quickly take his place, marching forward into direct fire. So moved was Confederate General Holtzclaw at witnessing their collective bravery, that the entry in his commander's field book from that day read, *"...such courage...they came only to die."*

Among the gallant men that day were two brothers, who were transplanted to middle Tennessee as slaves to work for ironmaster Montgomery Bell. John and Arch Nesbitt fought bravely alongside of their comrades at the Battle of Nashville and served admirably throughout the remainder of the war. The two brothers subsequently settled in the predominantly African American community of Promise Land, an optimistically named area just a few miles north of Charlotte, Tennessee, the county seat of Dickson County. They decided to make their home in a location within five miles of the Cumberland Furnace ironworks, where they once labored as slaves. Suffering from disabilities related to his service in the Civil War, John Nesbitt, appealed to the government for almost twenty years to secure the pension that he had been promised at the time of his admission into the Union Army. It was with help from these funds that the family later purchased land in the township and established the Promise Land School in the late 1880s. At the same time, the Edgewood School was educating white students just down the road at Ruskin Settlement. Promise Land School had the stated objective of assisting former slaves to acclimate more easily to freedom through education. The school performed that objective nobly, and continued to provide advancement through knowledge to its community until its closure in May 1956.

"Once let the black man get upon his person the brass letters U. S., let him get an eagle on his button and a musket on his shoulder and bullets in his pockets, and there is no power on earth which can deny that he has earned the right to citizenship in the United States." (Frederick Douglas)

By 1870, several dozen free black families owned in excess of one thousand combined acres in northern Dickson County. When most post-war black families were moving in droves into the industrialized areas of the north, the people of Promise Land decided to stay and cultivate a unique community in the rolling hills of middle Tennessee, the heart of the segregated south. As families took root, churches grew and people prospered. Promise Land hosted three church communities which included a Baptist Church, a Methodist Church, and an African Methodist Episcopal body of believers. The Promise Land School was widely supported throughout the community, and housed ninety-three students by 1905, with the two church buildings near the school acting as overflow space for the younger student population. At the height of the community's prominence, selected residents formed a gospel singing choir named the Promise Land Singers, whose performances at the local churches in the township were attended by mixed races; and as told to me by Pam's father, Augustus Scott, who attended several of these services as a youth, no evidence of race-related tensions were ever recorded.

The graveled Old Johnsonville Road ended at the water's edge at Pebble Isle Marina, where a prominently displayed small sailboat, mounted several feet from the ground, sat motionless on steel poles. I pulled into the parking lot where lines of beautiful boats of all kinds and makes were neatly stored in slips for the coming winter. Not a soul stirred anywhere that I could see. I continued along the road west, quickly arriving at the entrance of Johnsonville State Historic Park. The gate was open at the guard station but there was again no sign of a guard on duty, so I eased down the narrow paved road in the direction of the river. The landscape was hilly and covered in trees, ablaze with colors of red and yellow and brown. As I topped a small hill, I could see the wide expanse of blue water before me, captured in time against a row of Civil War era cannons which were staged against the embankment. A long earthen berm extended far into the river, assumed to be the remnants of the old rail line river crossing. In the distance, I could make out the pillars that once bore the trains on their shoulders as they made their way from Nashville to the final depot at Hickman, Kentucky.

The beauty of the scene before me was quietly captivating and filled me with emotions of gratitude and awe. A lone hawk crossed the sky in the distance, flying off across the river where Nathan Bedford Forrest and company shelled this Union train depot for days, men dying on both sides of a conflict that had no bearing on the outcome of the war. I moved in close to the cannons and leaned on one of the large wooden wheels. The air was brisk and smelled of cut timber. My eyes scanned out across the crystal waters of the Tennessee River, where reflections arose of the two men historically attached to this land, James and Nesbitt, whose lives I had traveled through to get here. My reflections upon the two distinctly different lives formed a perfect dichotomy about the choices we make given the experiences forced upon us by fate or invited by selection. One man started the war in bondage; the other man started the war in freedom. The free man left the war bound to his rage, while the bound man freed his soul to a greater goodness. As such, the slave became the freeman and the freeman the enslaved.

Ÿ

Johnsonville Depot on the Tennessee River

Chapter 9

« MIGRATION »

Crossing the new concrete bridge that replaced the old narrow steel truss structure at New Johnsonville into west Tennessee, I felt like a forgotten sojourner returning again to his homeland. It had been years since I visited this part of my home state, where as a youth I formulated the habits and beliefs of maturation that transformed a boy into a young man; that wonderful and horrible stage of *in-between-ness*, where the belief that the boy would rise to the responsibilities of the man depended greatly upon those responsibilities not falling too heavily or too quickly upon him. My family moved to west Tennessee during the summer of my first year in Junior High School. We remained in Jackson for longer than we lived anywhere in one place, which allowed me to graduate from Northside High School, before heading off to Clarksville for college. I never anticipated that my youthful experiences in places like Little Rock, Memphis, Brownsville, and Jackson would call to me again, but memories of times gone by now drew me like a moth to a candle. There was a strange stirring in my soul for reconnection, looking to find pieces of myself that I may have earlier left behind, probably because I wondered if the pieces were real. Determined to walk on that ground again, I was hoping that among the physical I would encounter the mystical, all the while knowing that things never stayed the same.

I cruised past the remnants of the old fish house east of Camden, our favorite Friday night eating destination during the two summers that I spent as a Boy Scout camp counselor at Camp Mack Morris. It was a rubble pile and unrecognizable. At the end of each week, the campers filed home in lines of single destination, leaving the counselors to roam the nearby town of tiny Camden looking for girls. We quickly learned that even with the local talent it was hard to attract much serious notice when all our clothes and hats were emblazoned with Boy Scout emblems. A few of the more experienced counselors selected from a deeper wardrobe of civilian clothes, including a bottle of Brut splash-on that was passed around and shared so much that we all smelled indistinguishable on town night. Despite noble efforts, it was hard to play the bad-boy role with young men that could each recite the twelve values of the Scout Law. Most of my time working at Camp Mack Morris was spent hanging out across the bay at Birdsong Marina, mingling through the campground and the dock store. It was during that first summer as a counselor that I became addicted to Mountain Dew and those little particles of citrus that floated around in the jade green bottle, characteristic of its early recipe. Dew and boats have stayed with me across all those years and it started there.

A few miles west of downtown Camden I crossed into Carroll County where the highway between the city and the old railroad town of Bruceton followed the historical NC & STL Railroad line. For years, the depots at Hollow Rock Junction, McKenzie and Huntingdon, were the main attractions for civic gatherings and the primary meeting locations for people headed to town. The aged depots were now forgotten and abandoned, but some remaining structures had been repurposed into small cafés or antique shops. An old and dear friend of mine, Marty Marshall, who passed into his eternal life just a few years ago, bought the abandoned depot in McKenzie, spending his personal time and money to restore it solely for the benefit of the community, and in recognition of his love for the Cumberland Presbyterian Church, and its flagship university, Bethel. Many years ago, when I heard from a mutual friend that Marty had purchased the structure, I called him and asked if it was true. He confirmed that indeed he had purchased the then dilapidated depot from the railroad, and when I inquired, *"Why?"* he responded, *"Why not?"* I lost touch with Marty and did not speak to him again for years due to my own neglect, hearing through mutual friends in Jackson about his unexpected passing on May 25, 2010. That wonderful and generous man spent as much time with me during the critical formative years of my life as did my own father, and he remained one of the finest people that God had placed into my earthly path.

The road through Carroll County, Tennessee followed the railroad line, purposefully connecting the larger cities of Nashville and Memphis across the state. By sheer luck of a straight vector, Huntingdon became a hub for being in the way. Before the railroad was plotted, the small community of McLemoresville served as the mainstay of this area's cultural, educational, and political activities. My Presbyterian ancestors on that branch of the family tree settled nearby, along a ridge near Cedar Grove community, where the forest was so thick that a man on a horse could barely pass through it.

I was in search of two cemeteries and ancestral remains, an Ulster line that started in Antrim County, Ireland, and led to Mint Hill, North Carolina, then Carroll County, Tennessee, and westward to Hardin Settlement in Arkansas. The first was Arthur Brown, the father of my mother's great-great grandmother Sarah Brown, and a Revolutionary War soldier, a resident of Carroll County, who was eighty-eight at the time of his death in 1849. The other ancestor was my mother's great-great grandfather, William Andrew Blair, the father of the first Blair buried in Arkansas soil, John W. Blair, a Union soldier that lived among predominantly Confederate neighbors. Both of these distant relatives had contributed their military and civic service toward the making of the two southern states, Arkansas and Tennessee, which had been my home since birth.

Farmers and laborers drawn from areas such as Carroll County, Tennessee made up the armies of men that made generals and politicians famous in history, and John Washington Blair was such a man. Along with his wife, Saphronia Bigham, and small first child, the Blair family dispatched themselves to the Hardin community of north-central Arkansas around 1856, following other members of the Bigham family, all seeking new horizons. They struggled greatly through a brutal winter that first year, living for weeks under the cover of only a wagon tent, and boiling dirt that they scratched from the ground for salt. At first opportunity, the new father erected a crude log cabin in the Narrows of the Black Fork Creek, where Blairs and Peels became neighbors, and soon after, family. Since the arrival of J. W. Blair, someone with the last name of Blair had lived on the land northeast of modern day Greenbrier, Arkansas without interruption for over 160 years.

When I was a boy, I would occasionally have the opportunity to visit my Blair cousins that lived along the Blair and Black Fork roads of this rocky area bordering Woolly Hollow State Park. One summer, my older cousin Joe Blair introduced me to a world of outdoor revelry and out-of-season deer hunting. I have never been an avid or enthusiastic hunter, but what red-blooded, southern American young man could turn down a chance to trample unsupervised through hundreds of acres of deciduous forest, carrying a loaded shotgun, drinking shots of whiskey straight from Uncle Bernard's stash, while chewing tobacco and talking about all things mystical and wonderful involving the opposite sex? The stories and possibilities opened up to me that week through the first hand experiences of my cousin Joe rang in my ears like tower bells, encouraging a world of potential pleasure and erogenous imagery that my mind could have never conceived prior to my visit. I was a child being introduced into a man's world; a lamb for the slaughter.

On a hot August day, Joe dragged me along to Woolly Hollow Lake, where two well-endowed young ladies had gathered to frolic in the swimming hole. One of the girls maintained an obvious existing relationship with my elderly cousin, as their warm up period was quickly completed. At this meeting, swimming seemed the least of their interests. The other young lady, slightly plump and not particularly attractive to me, allured me with her obvious desire for any outsider. I recalled being horrified at the prospect of having to perform at the level being established by Joe and his companion, so in a feeble attempt to hide my inexperience, I fumbled through the next two hours mimicking actions and interest for show, joking and hoping that the production would be enough to maintain some level of manly credibility. It was a summer of experience and terror.

Although my opportunities to visit Greenbrier were rare, I was always prompted of those memories of innocence and fear from that day on the lake, thankful now that back then I was too naïve to comprehend the full measure of responsibilities and challenges that awaited me down the road into true manhood. The old farm place still drew the Blairs and Peels every first weekend of June for the family reunion at Woolly Hollow State Park. The annual ritual of graveyard cleaning, storytelling, yarn spinning, hot dogs and potato salad sustains the mythologies of our ancestors for future generations, this story such an example.

Oddly, my growing up with God in so many ways mirrored my growing up with friends and family. Often times I sought His companionship with enthusiasm and need, while other times, I wanted to be left to learn some things on my own. I made promises to Him that I could not keep. I lied to Him about my intentions. I traded and bargained for favor when my own efforts of correction were exhausted. I tried to gain His favor by making commitments and promises outside of my ability to deliver. After my return from my summer visit with Cousin Joe, I vowed abstinence until marriage, horrified at the prospects of having to cross that bridge so early in my life. It was such a lofty thing to do as a teenager that I felt safe behind the weight of my promise. With this boundary now established, other boundaries were then opened to be explored. In my sophomore year of college, at the age of twenty, as inexperienced in life as almost anyone could be, I met Pam, and within a year, we were married. Clueless. Real life moved in with us quickly and I was wholly unqualified for it. Without any money, without having finished my education (which was free by the way because I was on a full academic scholarship), without any worldly experience, with little practical skills, with a limited world view, and an old, beat up Mercury Capri, Pam and I ran toward married life like two starving animals, both void of parental counseling that should have mounted strong exception to our decision. The dream of what we thought marriage would be lasted about two years, before the real world came to our door in the form of my leaving the family business in Arkansas, breaking my Dad's heart, and moving back to Tennessee, where I went to work selling god-forsaken life insurance, without an education and flat broke. I had traded the broken-down Capri for a Ford Pinto. That's how bad it was. Nothing brought reality to my door faster than trying to look like a successful insurance agent in a cheap suit and a cheaper car. When I told people in those days that I also did financial planning, it must have been from utter pity that they did not laugh right in my face, although some did. The decision to tell my father that I was quitting the business in Arkansas was the first of many times that I wished I could have avoided real manhood. I found the strength to make that decision, with reflection and love for my faith and my young wife, after several minutes of contemplation while visiting a headwater swamp in southeastern Arkansas, the Initial Point from which the lands of the Louisiana Purchase were measured. At least in that decision, I made the right choice.

Traveling south just outside Huntingdon, I turned onto the twisting Old Stage Coach Road that led to the Liberty All Methodist Church and Cemetery, a pristine white chapel structure with a working bell atop the eve of the front porch. In the southwest corner of the church, I noticed that the main floor beam was held aloft by a jagged piece of sandstone, a natural bolder that had been carved into the ground to make a flat spot upon which the load-bearing beam could rest. It was here that his loved ones put Revolutionary War veteran Arthur Brown to his rest in 1849. Brown enlisted in the Continental Army under Captain Thomas Armstrong in Pitt County North Carolina, where he then marched to Salisbury and joined the Continental Regiment under the command of Major Redding Blount of

Beaufort County. While serving in this capacity, the soldier and his unit joined with the Army of General Nathanael Greene at the High Hills of Santee. At the famous Battle of Eutaw Springs, the young soldier had a British bayonet run through his torso. He wore the scar until his death. Brown received medical care resulting in his honorable discharge from the Continental Army on April 15, 1782.

Almost forty years after his separation from service, Arthur Brown applied for a Revolutionary War pension, from which eight dollars per month was granted to him on June 23rd of 1818. Arthur married in North Carolina and migrated eventually to Carroll County, Tennessee, where one of his children, Sarah Brown, married Joseph Bigham, a pioneer to the area and person of wide and lasting respect to this day. The Bigham's would have many children, including a daughter named Sophronia, who married John Washington Blair on November 2, 1854 near McLemoresville. The couple made their way across the Mississippi River at Hickman Ferry and put down roots into north-central Arkansas east of Greenbrier, a location near the Hardin community outside of Enola, founded by Jonathan Hardin, the son of Joab and Sarah. My great, great grandparents lived there until their deaths.

The Liberty All cemetery in Carroll County was wonderfully kept by what was clearly a loving attention to the souls buried there. I walked from row to row, looking down at the names of the people that lived in this community for decades. Time was no respecter of status, as death fell upon the old and the young, but in a place such as this, so far removed from the hustle of society and the demands of our labors, there was a peace that took hold of me and a quiet joy warmed my soul. A silent voice on one of the tombstones encouraged *"a race well run,"* another life judged well lived. The dead lived again every time we spoke their names aloud. I called out my father's name, *"Roy Glenn Hall,"* into the wind and stood quietly wondering if I would hear an answer; the hurt of so many years without a father to lean on. Images of my own mortality, closer now than ever before, gathered around me like a shroud. I knew at that moment that I must write what was in my heart, so that my children could read it, follow me here someday chasing the same ghosts, and know their father through these words, and call my name aloud into the wind.

Leaving Liberty All Cemetery, I followed the Old Stage Road south until it merged with McLemoresville Road, and then turned back east for a few miles, crossing over Highway 70 into what was left of the community of Cedar Grove, where at the junction of two old wagon roads stood the New Liberty Baptist Church and the New Liberty Cemetery. This was the resting place of my grandmother's great grandfather, William Andrew Blair, who settled into Carroll County, Tennessee sometime before the census of 1840. There was little that our family knew about this particular person except a few vague details handed down to my grandmother Ruth. We knew that despite their Tennessee home, they were Union sympathizers.

Admittedly, as a boy, hearing that my great-great-grandfather was a Yankee soldier greatly challenged my southern sensibilities. In the bright light of revealed history, however, this fact now  imparted a certain pride. John W. Blair, the very son of the man whose grave I was now seeking, had summoned the courage to enlist as a soldier into the 3rd Cavalry, Company G, of General Frederick Steele's VII Corps Union Army of Arkansas after they captured Little Rock in September of 1863. I bore no inclination of condemning those in my family who alternatively served with the Confederates in defense of their homeland, but what remained confounding to my sensibilities was the unending clamor of southern sympathizers of subsequent generations who spoke so poetically about honor and valor in remembrance of those most directly responsible for the atrocities of the war. The beneficiaries of the enslavement of others deserve no such honor that continues to be celebrated on the landscape of the modern South where I make my home. It's long past time to take down the flag and bury the false pride. News flash: we lost, and thank God.

"Our progress into degeneracy appears to me to be pretty rapid. As a nation, we began by declaring that "all men are created equal". We now practically read it "all men are created equal, except negroes." (Abraham Lincoln, 1855, in a personal letter to Joshua Speed, a friend and slave owner)

On the very ground where I stood, during the brutal winter of 1862, passed the marauding Confederate General Nathan Bedford Forrest and his contingent of men, winding down their expedition into West Tennessee. Here, he encountered the pursuing brigades of Colonels Cyrus L. Dunham and John W. Fuller at Parkers Crossroads. Forrest's troops took the early advantage by attacking Dunham before Fuller's soldiers had arrived. Upon Fuller's later surprise attack from the north, Forrest blasted through the demoralized southern line of Dunham's brigade and headed south toward the Tennessee River, escaping with limited casualties despite being totally hemmed in on all sides by the Union army. This battle and dozens of other stories created the lore that surrounded Nathan Bedford Forrest's reputation in southern history and literature, as exemplified by the state park north of Camden that bears his name. Widely recognized as one of the most brilliant military strategists of the Confederacy, he was also one of the more prominent figures in the formation of the Ku Klux Klan immediately after the war and served as its "Grand Wizard" until 1869. Prior to the war, Forrest owned hundreds of slaves across several plantations based in West Tennessee and enriched himself through a slave trading enterprise headquartered in downtown Memphis. Forrest's reputation as a warrior was well earned given his battlefield aggressiveness in total dedication to the institution of slavery, and the wealth and privilege that free labor had afforded him from his childhood beginnings in poverty.

The harsh brutality of the man also left a history of its own, given his leadership role in one of the most tarnished episodes of the Civil War, the Fort Pillow Massacre; a Mississippi River fortress located north of Memphis, Tennessee. History recorded the mass brutality focused upon black captured Union soldiers, the vast majority of whom it was later determined had been killed by enraged Forrest-commanded Confederates after their surrender, in what historian Richard Fuchs, author of *An Unerring Fire*, called "an orgy of death – a mass lynching to satisfy the basest of conduct – intentional murder – for the vilest of reasons – racism and personal enmity." Nevertheless, at the Nathan Bedford Forrest State Park about twenty miles east of the cemetery, among the many amenities were camping areas, the most popular of which, Happy Hollow Campground, offered nearly forty beautifully wooded sites equipped with tables, grills, water, and electrical hookups. A large silver medallion of the Confederate General full astride his galloping horse greeted every visitor to the park since its establishment in 1929.

It was odd that I would end up so close to this location through the journeys of my own life. I considered north Jackson, Tennessee my home, a location not more than twenty-five miles from this cemetery. I never knew about my relatives living in this area until I was well into middle age, yet again encircled by the concentric rings of life experience that kept showing themselves through the mystical patterns of time and space. In Jackson, during my high school years, my Dad and I would often fish not far down the road, at Maple Creek Lake, a small lake located inside of Natchez Trace National Forest. It was a special place for me, and over the years as occasion allowed me to pass by the park on Interstate 40, I would often take the 5-mile, 10-minute side journey over to the lake in remembrance of times there with my

Dad. Knowing now that my ancestors had also reached their hands into this same dirt made my memories of days at Maple Creek Lake even more special and more profound.

After looking for several minutes without finding the headstone of William Andrew Blair, I turned back toward my pickup and the church parking lot, ready to leave New Liberty Cemetery to the dead among the old cedar trees that shaded the majority of the plots. The birds were playing in the cemetery, swooping down to and fro among the old stones, and then back into the trees lining the boundary of the property, oblivious to my intrusion and the history of lives that lay beneath their flight paths. I stepped as carefully as I could among the rows of dead in honor of their graves. I wondered if my grandfathers had times of ease like this moment, just to drift and watch the birds and wonder. It was most probable that young John Blair joined his father along this very road to town, never knowing the legacy that he would leave and that I now joined. It was hard to put into words, but standing where my ancestors had stood before me, and realizing how close my path followed theirs, I could only believe that the decisions that we make in our lives are somehow attached to one another across the generations by a mystical cord, an unseen overseer, joined as a spirit to the same physical blood that once ran through their veins, and now mine. Blood was the eternity of this physical realm. As long as subsequent life was born from it, it never died – we never died. I could see that very truth taking place here, below the ancient cedars that shaded the graves and among the difficult lives that had come before me, and now rested. I lived only because they lived. It was a humbling reflection. There was no reason to spend so much of my life's precious time in fear and dread. My orbit was secure, and things would be what they would be, and that was as it should be.

Ÿ

Fog bank rolling over the Ohio River near Smithland, Kentucky

Chapter 10

« CROSSING OVER »

All of the towns along my route following the Ohio River grew from the great expansion of immigrants into what was then the western edge of American civilization. A few of the towns turned themselves into vibrant cities, adjusting well to the changing patterns of life and transportation that defined the places where people wanted to live versus the places where they had to live. The early settlers of western Kentucky must have spent a lot of time praying that the water levels of the Cumberland, Tennessee, and Ohio rivers would hold against the levees they constructed, as all three great bodies of water emptied onto one another within a few miles of this location. It was a unique area of our country where rivers joined, land shifted, and people determined to find new adventures and new beginnings pressed themselves across it all despite the odds.

Having spent the night in Paducah, I woke early and headed north along the riverbank toward the historic town of Smithland, a much smaller community than expected. Lining the town's narrow roads were homes, once distinguished, but now barely standing. A couple of the historic houses had been saved from the ravages of time and still stood in the midst of their original splendor, but several other grand river homes of earlier days stood lonely, awaiting their ultimate, final fate of the bulldozer. Numerous empty lots dotted the small squares of narrow roads that framed the old, bawdy river town against the channel, hinting at homes once filled with large and happy families now abandoned. Newer, non-descript civic buildings that looked lost and inappropriate, like a concession stand in the middle of a graveyard, were erected for the important business of the government. All of the reasons that people flocked to this location at the beginning of the 1800s were gone, and all of the reasons that people fled, remained. The river fishermen were the only residual constant.

I took a brief walk along the high bluffed river road, watching personal fishing boats launch into the calm bay, the still water shedding the weight of early morning mist against the rising sun. Being near and on the water had always given me a special peace like nothing else, and I loved all boats of any kind and any shape, having secured that first love as a youth at scout camp. Toward the north, the bay was wide and ominous, as the mouth of the Cumberland converged with the flowing Ohio. It seemed certain that the great body of water could impose its will against this small town whenever it chose to do so. Flooding had haunted the town since its beginnings in the late 1700s, when the lusty river town was first established. By 1810, the town began to attract settlers from the east headed west, hoping to find cheap and rich farmlands upon which to toil their fortunes, and that was when the Peels came down from Virginia. Like them, pioneers from all points back east poured into the area, always pushing the boundaries farther and farther into Indian lands, and the Native Americans

Lucy Jefferson memorial DAR erected, near Smithland, Kentucky

farther and farther into the wilderness, not waiting on the rule of law to catch up with them. Only the river temporarily slowed them here, as the government continued lying to the Tribes through Land Treaties for decades, meaningless agreements designed to steal property that the organized states considered uninhabited land from the outset.

Returning to my vehicle, I drove a few miles north across the Cumberland River looking for one of those settler families, the plantation home of Lucy Jefferson, the sister of our renowned President Thomas Jefferson. I had read that a monument was erected in her honor by the Daughters of the American Revolution near her Kentucky home and burial location. Crossing the narrow steel bridge bearing her name, I entered the small township where her husband, Charles Lilburn Lewis, dragged the family away from comfortable surroundings in Virginia because of failing fortunes, and obtained several hundred acres of land with assistance from the government, ostensibly in continued recognition of his family's military service during the American Revolution. The fact that he was the brother-in-law of Thomas Jefferson probably did not impede the argument of a sizable land grant in the unchartered territory of western Kentucky. Furthermore, Charles was a cousin of Meriwether Lewis, the renowned adventurer and co-captain of the Corps of Discovery expedition, both natives of Albemarle County, Virginia. Charles served the new country as a Colonel in the American Revolution alongside of his father, Charles Lewis of Buck Island, and in return, was granted this sizable partial of land bordering the mighty Ohio River.

For most of his life, the acclaimed Colonel Lewis fared well back east; however, as he approached sixty years of age, the family's good fortune took a turn south. Charles and Lucy, along with their three grown sons and daughters, decided to move west to Kentucky hoping to improve their run of bad luck, and settled in 1806, near Berry's Ferry, the most popular place to cross the Ohio River into Golconda, Illinois (most notably as the northern route of the Trail of Tears). They aptly named the place, *Rocky*

Hill Plantation, where the family grew cotton, feed and root crops, and raised livestock using slave labor to till the fertile, but frequently flooded, river plain. By 1811, the family's hopes for better times in the west had dissolved. During that year, the Colonel lost his oldest son Randolph, his daughter-in-law, Lilburn's wife, and most tragic of all, the untimely death of his beloved Lucy. Despondent from what seemed to be an endless thread of tragedy, Charles Lewis slipped further into bleakness, leaving his remaining two sons charged with looking after the family affairs, which included families and farms of their own, all barely making it. Now up against the western border of civilization, they were out of room to run away any farther.

The two living brothers, Isham and Lilburn, were angry and bitter at life. On a dark night in December of 1811, older brother Lilburn, in a drunken rage, murdered a 17-year old slave named George in front of the other household slaves, killing him with a hand axe. Younger brother Isham was staying at Lilburn's home for an extended visit and witnessed the savage act through his state of inebriation. The slave's error was an accident. He had dropped and broken a water pitcher that belonged to the brothers' deceased mother. Lilburn's rage boiled against the African American youth, and when the hacking was completed, he ordered the horrorstruck household witnesses to cover up the event by further chopping up the body of George and burning it in the house chimney, piece by piece. Despite the wide proliferation of slave ownership in 1811, it was illegal to kill a slave in Kentucky without provocation. If not for a bizarre set of confounding circumstances which occurred within hours of the event, history may have never recorded the heinous act.

After midnight, on December 16, 1811, while the body of young George was being burned in the fireplace of the Lewis home, the New Madrid Earthquake struck the Kentucky area with a force of nature incomprehensible to its residents. Most who experienced the series of large tremors believed that the end of the world was at hand. As if God himself had ordained justice for the slave George, the earthquake shook the stones from the Lewis family chimney where his body had been stuffed, leaving charred body parts in plain sight among the rubble. After the initial tremor subsided, the Lewis brothers quickly hid the undisposed parts beneath the brick pile that remained. Some days later, Lilburn instructed slaves to rebuild the fallen chimney, inside of which they again enclosed the remaining charred body parts of George; however, God would not be trifled with. In the aftermath of several residual earthquakes which continued into January and February of 1812, the chimney hiding the body of the murdered young man became dislodged for a second time, and this time with his skull showing up in clear view on the main road, dragged there by the Lewis dogs. The skull was found by a passerby and turned into the local authorities for investigation.

In the inquiry that followed the discovery of the skull, both brothers were charged with the murder of slave George. Lilburn, unable to bear the weight of his circumstances and already reeling under a cloud of despondency, committed suicide prior to his trial and while released on bail. Isham Lewis escaped the area, with obvious assistance of local sympathizers, never to be heard from again, his fate remaining lost to history to this day. Some verbal accounts of Isham Lewis purported his migration back east, only to be subsequently killed in the War of 1812. The Madrid Earthquake signaled an end to the Lewis family in Kentucky and the beginning of the Peel family in Arkansas. The few remaining Lewis members headed back east while the Peels pushed even farther west.

Driving across the bridge when returning to Paducah, I was somewhat haunted by the story of the Lewis brother's murder of the young man George, and the insanity that overcame them. It was as if the light went out on the family when the influence of their mother was no longer there to instill her virtues into their respective lives. The strands of influence of a single good life could stretch across many souls and even into subsequent generations. As easily as one could stumble upon evil, goodness, when found, should be nurtured and cherished, honored and protected. Only a few minutes earlier, I was staring at the concrete monument commemorating the life of their mother, Lucy Jefferson, whose claim to history was that she was the sister of her famous sibling. Brother Thomas was destined for historical exaltation, while Lucy was remembered through a legacy of shame. In some ways, Lucy Jefferson's personal and private life may have been better lived than her famous brother's, although history had already decided not to tell it that way. History, after all, is written by people. We record a lot of what we want to remember and leave out a lot of what we hope to forget.

I bid adieu to the Jefferson family and headed west toward the mighty Mississippi. Upon reaching the town of Wickliffe, I turned north along the Great River Road, a pathway so overgrown with foliage and vegetation that it seemed like a road going to nowhere. Suddenly, the majestic body of water revealed itself out from the undergrowth and a brilliantly wide sky filled up my truck windshield. I maneuvered the sharp left turn onto the viaduct which approached the magnificent steel structure that spanned the hurried Ohio. The early afternoon sun peeked over the top portion of the massive steel girding, and mirrored reflections dotted portions of the bridge at different angles like a kaleidoscope. The sound of my tires rolling over the uneven steel floor gratings made a rotating humming sound that changed pitch between sections and tossed my pickup in small but quick swaying movements from side to side. More modern bridges were designed for wider traffic and well fitted with an emergency pull-off lane, but this old beauty was a vintage of an earlier time, its narrow lanes crossing a long span with no room for error on either side. It was marvelous and regal in design and glowed with an elegant aesthetic far beyond its utility value. Crossing the mighty Ohio on the back ridge of this steel lady was an adventure in and of itself. In due time, I knew all of these old bridges formed from girded steel and rivets would be gone forever, and my grandchildren would probably never have the experience of driving across something so exquisitely envisioned and experienced.

At the end of the Ohio River Bridge, I made a sharp left turn onto the Scenic Byway to cross the mighty Mississippi, where I anticipated that a similar and wonderful experience awaited me. My eagerness of this crossing was not always so welcomed to others, and the contrast was never more apparent to me as haunting images from the documentary, *Children of the Camps*, suddenly flashed into my mind, and recollection of the role played by Arkansas' favorite daughter, Hattie Caraway, in support of the internment of Japanese Americans during World War II. During her teenage years, Ruth Asawa lived happily and comfortably with her family in California. She dreamed of becoming an artist. Arkansas' Senator Hattie Caraway was an outspoken advocate of Japanese internment and heavily lobbied the War Department to establish two camps along the Mississippi River in the Arkansas delta. Camp Jerome and Camp Rohwer at their peaks held nearly 20,000 Japanese-American citizens as censured prisoners of their own government. Ruth's family was assigned to Camp Rohwer, taken from their home in California, bused initially to Memphis for processing, and then driven by military escort across the Mississippi River to the sweltering camp located near the diminutive community of Duce, Arkansas. Where my family crossed into Arkansas into a hopeful future, young Ruth Asawa crossed the river below me into captivity, guilty of nothing except being born Japanese in a paranoid America. It was from this deep experience of moral injustice that the artist later in life found the inspiration to capture the beautiful and the fanciful through her unique and inspiring sculptures. Asawa was responsible for the design of many sculptures and fountains of distinction across her native California, including the famous *Andrea's Fountain of Mermaids* near the entrance of Ghirardelli Square in San Francisco, where happy children play in its mist. I once sat at its edge on a beautiful bay day and ate a heavenly bar of orange-laced chocolate, square by square, savoring my freedom and thinking of home.

The old steel bridge across the Mississippi River seemed recently painted and somewhat less ominous than the bridge spanning the Ohio. There was no barge activity that I could see, but only a wide expanse of flowing water across a broad sand plain, along which sandbars had been constructed for safe anchoring of the river's traffic. I was thrilled at the experience of crossing these famous rivers at this historic location, and wondered if that same sense of amazement filled my ancestors at their crossing. It had to have been a once in a lifetime experience for them because arrival on the western side meant that the cord of their wilderness boundary was severed and only the unknown, and hope, lay out before them. Once across the river, whatever the experience to accomplish it, moving forward was their only viable destination – always forward from here on. I trained my eyes toward the west while topping the arch of the tapered bridge. West was the direction of dreams, certainly then and perhaps now as well. At the crest of the far horizon, I strained to find the outline of the distant Ozarks in the shadows of the clouds, and I could feel the allure of their presence.

Andrea's Fountain, Fisherman's Wharf, San Francisco, California

Champion Arkansas Bald Cypress, White River National Wildlife Refuge, Ethel, AR

Chapter 11

« BLACK RIVER »

"They watched the tide bring in a brittle, dimpled, breaking flood of silver through his skin, then open up his glistening eyes in which they saw their fear rise up to greet them one last time and fade, and disappear; disappear while they stood back like mourners round a grave, and watched his life ebb out of theirs, wave by wave by wave." (Poet Andrew Motion, UK, *The Field of Mirrors*)

It was hard to know what motivation or madness drove someone to pack up all that they owned, load it onto a rickety wagon, and head out into an unknown wilderness, crossing miles and miles of undeveloped trails in dangerous territory. The excitement from having just crossed the confluence of the two mighty rivers at Cairo prefaced my sense of awe for those early explorers, as the unique expansiveness of the plains of the Mississippi River lay out before me. A person looking for solitude could easily get lost inside of all of this space. I traveled on a dead straight line through the almost desolate Bootheel of Missouri from New Madrid to Malden with no distractions other than my thoughts. To conquer this land mass, settlers systematically drained the swamps, cut the timber, and dug irrigation canals that crisscrossed the open plains like a wire mesh. The land was rich and vibrant for plant growth, drawing its bounty from centuries of nutrients deposited by the frequent flooding of the water arteries that fed the river vein from the east.

There was complete emptiness across the imposing horizons, broken only by corrugated metal grain bins, tractor sheds, and concrete slab homes of the dispersed residents, and the crops that grew in resplendent lines from the earth. At some vistas, I could see for miles across the fields. The scene reminded me of my overseas travels in The Netherlands, where the canals were as inextricably associated with the land as were its famous windmills. There, as here, I was captivated by the majesty of nothingness and the beauty of the void. I thought about the millions across our country that would never experience the total freedom of being so splendidly away from everything and everybody.

At the time of the beginning of the great migration into the Arkansas territory in the early 1800s, millions of acres of land were unfit for cultivation given the volatility of the river systems at that time. Vast stands of bald-cypress and water tupelo trees, often as thick as six feet across the center, were scattered across the untouched prehistoric land. Pioneers struggled to establish homesteads among the heavily timbered forest and utilized the abundant wood for home building, fuel, and furnishings. Often times the clearing of crop fields and stock pastures took years to complete, as the farmers, like undeterred ants, systematically chopped away at the great stands of trees to make room for the civilization they brought with them. As demand in the east increased for wood barrels, crates, axe handles, and a myriad of other wood products, companies such as the Brooklyn Cooperage Company and H. S. Williams Cooperage Co. moved into the area to pillage the vast forest resources unabated. In the few decades between the arrival of the timber robbers and the railroads, the land had been all but emptied of its primordial forest, and like swarms of human locusts, they continued their path of clear-cutting deep into the center of the Ozarks until the big trees were exhausted. There were only a handful of these giant monoliths remaining across the state to testify to the carnage, tucked away in places where the axe-men failed to find them. I read that one such giant remained in the forest of White River National Wildlife Refuge, and I had it in my mind to someday see the big tree, a survivor of the lost race of ancients. From Popular Bluff, Missouri to Leslie, Arkansas in the center of the Ozark range, the swath of unsustainable butchery from the saw blade and axe eventually raped the mountains and swamps of their virgin forest, and then predictably, the loggers packed up and pulled out of town, carrying their once favored jobs with them, and leaving no residual planting behind; only stumps left to rot over time where kings of the forest once stood.

Beginning in the Bootheel of Missouri and framing a western slanted arch down to the city of Helena was Crowley's Ridge, the natural barrier anomaly of loess sediment along which the earliest pioneers built settlements in protection of the disruptive flood waters of the Mississippi River. The ground along this ridge, deposited by ancient glaciers, accumulated across the centuries from windblown piles to form the separation barrier between the plains and the rivers. The cities of Piggott, Rector, Paragould, Jonesboro, Harrisburg, Wynne, Forrest City, Marianna, and Helena traced the north-south boundary of the geological formation that rose some 250 to 550 feet above the Mississippi plain in the shape of a quarter-moon. Given the condition of the uncultivated land and the looming flood plain, it was no mistake that vast areas of eastern Arkansas had so few people living there. The field notes of the Louisiana Purchase surveyor Joseph Brown, moving west from his starting point north of modern day Helena, Arkansas, noted time and time again the natural disposition of the swamp-covered land: "level and very wet...green briers and

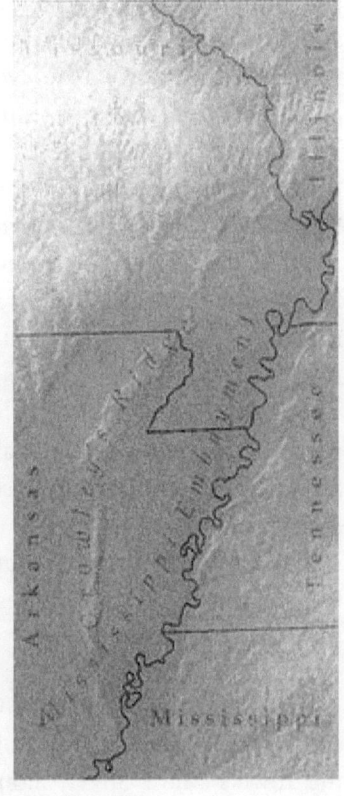

vines." The geological rise of Crowley's Ridge in the northeastern portion of the state provided just enough land elevation from the swamplands and oxbow lakes to afford reliable transportation and crop fortification. It was the well-traveled path along this ridge that garnered the majority of the land-based settlement traffic into central Arkansas via Tennessee and southern Kentucky. Pioneers entering the territory from Missouri expanded the utilization of the ancient Natchitoches Trace Indian trail, turning it into the legendary white man's Southwest Trail. One migration path followed the outer land ridge while the other followed the inland rivers, merging with one another in the valleys of the mountain ranges.

The earliest migration into the territory began in the south of the state with the establishment of Arkansas Post along the Arkansas River and then moved inward. As safer and more predictable river traffic became available, migration patterns similarly hugged the intermittently navigable Black and White rivers flowing down from western and central Missouri. The confluence of these two minor rivers at the pioneer town of Jacksonport provided one of the early points of origin from where travelers moving farther west or north could obtain provisions for the remainder of their journey. I planned a route that would roughly follow the southwestern migration route of the Peel family down into north-central Arkansas, beginning at the joined rivers at Cairo, where I had just crossed, and then zig-zaging myself between the Crowley's Ridge and the old Southwest Trail. There was no oral or written history of exactly how the Peels, and the other fifteen families that accompanied their journey from Smithland, Kentucky, traversed the 300 miles. With only two days available for exploration before meeting up with Danny at Bull Shoals, I committed to making the most of this opportunity to explore a bit of both routes, knowing that I would be pushing time chasing history.

At the far north end of Crowley's Ridge, I approached the small and unassuming town of Piggott. Within a stone's throw of the town's Main Street, along a normal lane that looked like thousands of similar neighborhood streets throughout the south, I came upon a nicely kept, but certainly non-imposing, two-story Hardy-board home once owned by one of the wealthiest people in Arkansas. Paul Pfeiffer was one of three heirs of the vast Warner-Lambert pharmaceutical empire, but instead of remaining in the family's home town of Saint Louis, Paul decided to make a permanent home in the farming country of Piggott, about a two hour drive south, in the upper northeastern corner of Arkansas. In pursuit of a lifelong dream for a simple but productive life, Paul and his devoted wife Mary, left behind the Saint Louis based company business and the moved 150 miles, assuming the role of gentleman farmer and lady gardener. Paul's older brother, Gus, took over the reins of the family's vast business empire, soon moving the headquarters to New York City, and then later selling the sprawling Warner-Lambert group of companies to Pfizer Corporation, thus enabling the generations of Pfeiffer family philanthropy that continued to support the medical sciences and the arts to this day.

Purchasing over 60,000 acres of adjoining highlands and lowlands just outside of Piggott, Paul and Mary quickly became one of the most prominent families in the state, as well as having the distinction of being the in-laws of American writer, Ernest Hemingway. At the time of their arrival into Piggott, their grown daughter, Pauline, worked as a column writer for the ladies' magazine *Vanity Fair* based in Paris, France. It was there that she met a dashing, although married, writer named Ernest Hemingway. In time, Hemingway would leave his first wife for the hand of the young heiress and settle down with Pauline in Paris. While the Pfeiffer's eventually grew to appreciate the talents of their new son-in-law, their personal Christian faith was significantly challenged knowing that their daughter was involved with Hemingway while he was married. Especially troubling for Mary Pfeiffer, an ardent Catholic, was realizing that Pauline contributed to Hemingway's divorce from his first wife, also a Saint Louis native, the evocative Hadley Richardson, who was the mother of Hemingway's son, John Nicanor. In an odd, but perhaps predictable, move to appease his new in-laws,

Hemingway converted his faith to Catholicism prior to his marriage to Pauline, most likely to keep the trust fund checks coming.

'For many months I have been asking our Heavenly Father to make the crooked ways straight and your life's pathway one of peace and happiness, and this morning. I feel a quiet assurance that my prayers have not been in vain..." (Letter from Mary Pfeiffer to Pauline, May 10, 1927; source: *Arkansas Catholic*)

Hemingway frequented his in-laws home in Piggott for occasional extended visits of writing and relaxation. Heavily dependent upon the Pfeiffer's wealth for his financial support during this time, the majority of the locals of Piggott, themselves hard-working and sacrificial people, viewed Hemingway with much consternation and widely considered him a beatnik and a gold-digger. Whatever time the yet-to-be-famous writer spent in Arkansas was clearly intentioned toward keeping his rich wife happy. He had few good words to say about the state and its heat.

"His helmet now shall make a hive for bees; and lover's sonnets turned to holy psalms, a man-at-arms must now serve on his knees, and feed on prayers, which are Age his alms." (A Farewell to Arms [to Queen Elizabeth], George Peele)

The couple had two children together before their divorce thirteen years later, when in keeping with his pattern, Hemingway traded in his current St. Louis wife who formerly worked for *Vogue* magazine, and had rich parents, for another St. Louis woman of prominence, Martha Gellhorn, a renowned war correspondent, who oddly enough also worked for *Vogue*, and oddly enough also had family money. The Pfeiffer's two-story frame home, and renovated garage writer's shop that the family constructed specifically for Hemingway's use, was now an Arkansas Historical Site open to the public. The Hemingway-Pfeiffer Museum, a name which provided the ex-son-in-law top billing for a property he did not pay to construct, did not own, and rarely used, was a visitor's anomaly to this otherwise inconsequential rural Arkansas farm town, which continued to benefit from the efforts of the Pfeiffer Educational Center funded from the family's trust. Hemingway never left a dime on any doorstep of Piggott. By the end of his life, Earnest Hemingway married a total of four women, and at the end fell into extremely poor health, exasperated by his chronic drinking and otherwise excessive living. He exited life at the end of a shotgun barrel at age 62. Pauline Pfeiffer never remarried.

Leaving Piggott, I headed west on U.S. Highway toward Pocahontas, determined to set my own eyes upon the infamous Pocahontas Meteorite, which purportedly fell from a fiery sky in July of 1859 and landed just outside of town near the bank of the Black River. The large stone was subsequently found by local farmer, A. H. Keith, and remained in the care of his family for over 100 years, until then donated to the city of Pocahontas, where it was now proudly displayed near the downtown court square, sitting outside, on a concrete slab protected by a small metal fence. The drive across the high plains exposed the undulating terrain of the plateau that separated the lowlands and highlands of the state. Along the backside of Crowley's Ridge, the land rolled in soft curves where square bales of hay littered the freshly cut pastures of bluestem grass and clover. I rolled down my window in order to smell the aroma from the freshly cut grass. The hilly terrain was short lived. By the time I reached the unincorporated communities of Pollard and McDougal, I was again overtaken by vast tracts of flatlands, where soybean and corn crops bent their heads for miles following the afternoon sun. In this area, the diagonal line of cultural and geographic disparity began, setting a southwestern vector from here to the far corner of the state where Texas and Arkansas shared the boundary of the ever-twisting path of the Red River.

The people of these pioneer communities existed in a cultural ether, a brew of conflicting values and dichotomies of religious fever, political extremism, and drunken debauchery somehow molded into a justified religion. Belonging demanded self-sufficiency and cultural compliance, and the early settlers saw no hypocrisy between their religious zeal and their intolerance of anything or anyone different. Many of the more hot-blooded, clan-serving individuals bound themselves up with untenable commitments of pride rooted in perpetual conflict with their neighbors or strangers who dared to tread on their viewpoint. One thing that most hill families held onto, above all else, was a grudge. The forbearers expected that a family grudge would extend for decades and be honored by multiple future generations. Forgiveness was granted to appease God, but forgetting was fanatically ignored. Many of the rambunctious settlers were societal malcontents, picking up families and livestock, and moving them with little notice based upon an overheard conversation of opportunity elsewhere, or some grievance with friend or foe at their present location. The hill people could be very neighborly, but their attitude could change very quickly. It was education, ceded into the hills over generations of time, which helped turn the tide of ignorance and intolerance, the wisdom of which still failed some people who remained trussed to this land. Other families in northern Arkansas had finally learned that all things alike were not necessarily all things good.

George Chevrie dreamed of a better life in the wild territory of Arkansas. Prior to 1900 and hopeful to find work, he moved his family just outside downtown Pocahontas from Michigan. While farmers, like my family, dominated the landscape, there were actually occupations that were considered lower than farming, and George Chevrie had one of those jobs. He was a river fisherman. George scrapped a bad living from selling catfish, mussels, and eels caught along the muddy bank waters of the Black and White Rivers. Adding insult to injury, the Chevrie's could not afford housing in town and lived in a corrugated tin shed that was lashed to a narrow barge and tied to cypress trees lining the riverbank. Any heavy rain would threaten to dislodge their home from its makeshift moorings, so a constant, nervous vigil was required.

The *"barge people"* occupied a row of shanties just north of the Marr Creek Bridge. The adults and children endured the unsanitary conditions prevalent at a time when water usage for whatever reason was unencumbered. In 1901, the river was any man's passageway to use as he saw fit, and frequently loggers would float their cut timber down the river unattended, whereby a person downstream would be positioned to fetch the bundles of logs out of the river at a predetermined takeout point. These logs intermingled with livestock, boats, and natural debris, all of which posed their own hazards. It was not unusual, therefore, that accidents related to the chaotic commerce of river traffic were common. Such an accident was brought to bear upon the Chevrie family during the Spring of 1901 when their small barge shack was hit by loose logs free-floating down the Black River toward the sawmill. That's when the trouble started for a desperate and hopeless man.

I had seen my own days of desperation, although not from causes based in the sufferings of my children. That level of anguish carries its own, unique brand of horror. Our personal fortunes did struggle for many years. Pam and I worked our fingers to the bone to try and maintain a decent roof over our heads and ensure our children's university educations. When my father died suddenly in 1983, I had already dropped out of college in the winter of 1980 to join him in the business in El Dorado. I left behind an academic scholarship that paid for my tuition, books, and assisted with housing expenses. I was basically going to college at that time for free. It was dumb then and even worse looking back on it.

My decision to leave Austin Peay so abruptly burdened my life for years. It all fixed itself in later years, with Pam's help, mutual toil and sacrifice, a lot of driving, a ton of coffee, and large student loans. The process was made excruciating instead of enjoyable because of my own early poor decisions. I cannot say with certainty that all decisions made in haste were bad, but in my recollections, I can think of few that were good. I eventually completed college, earned two master's degrees, and ultimately completed my educational journey with a doctorate conferred in 2010. Without Pam helping me and sacrificing for my benefit all those years through all those classes, it would have never happened. It only worked when we decided to do things together and equally shared in the burdens and the benefits.

I pulled into the Black River Overlook Park at the edge of Pocahontas, and walked for a few minutes around the circular track to the edge of the flowing river. It was a bright, fresh day and whiffs of spices from the nearby Mexican restaurant drifted past my nose, reminding me of my held hunger. The grounds were beautiful and well-kept and afforded a great view of the river, which was flowing mildly around the bend toward the steel bridge. A hundred years earlier, this was a muddy spot of ground low enough to the river's edge to be flooded regularly, and there were clear indications that flooding still occurred. In the days of George Chevrie, there was a small bridge crossing Marr Creek which drained into the river beside the park, near the same location of the newer concrete bridge crossing. For generations most of the locals knew this bridge as the *"Red Bridge,"* simply because it had been painted red by local authorities. Unlike today, where I was the only walker on the path that encircled the park's perimeter, in March of 1901, this entire park and surrounding area was filled with onlookers, peering sanctimoniously at the swinging body of George Chevrie, the river fisherman, hanging from the rafters of the Red Bridge.

The man was a murderer and had shot a deputy in cold blood the day earlier for trying to cut loose from his possession a group of logs which floated down river and crashed into his tattered barge home. In those stray logs, George saw a way to put some food on his table other than catfish. Besides, one of his children, the third girl, Blanche, had been sick for months the year earlier and died in September. The family was unable to afford proper medical care for the ill child and was forced to watch her precious life slip away while other children from more prominent families were cared for. Life in Pocahontas was brutally hard until then for the Chevrie's, but after the death of young Blanche, her father's favorite, it had become even harder. His grief was irreconcilable, and it was somebody's fault that nobody tried to help them. Also, the spring rains were threatening the stability of his river-borne home on almost a weekly basis, and fishing had turned bad. Even when there were good catches, there was not enough demand to warrant a fair wage from his efforts. When the errant logs came crashing into his home, George quickly gathered them up intending to resell them before the owner took notice. It was only three or four logs. To him, they looked like food for his family. Some people in the community took notice of George's new collection before he could remove them to the mill and encouraged Marshal John Morris to collect and return the missing logs to their rightful owner.

George initially refused to comply with the Marshal's request to cut loose the logs and then demanded payment for the damages done by the floating timber to his shack. If he could not confiscate the property, then he would try and extort a ransom from it. He was not about to let this opportunity escape even a meager advantage for his family, and his demand for reparations were merely a cry for help from a desperate man who had exhausted all of his will and energy in a world that hardly noticed his pain. The Marshal, sensing that timing was bad for this discussion, left George to think about it overnight and told him to have the logs cut loose for the owner by the next morning. A good night's sleep should have resulted in wiser heads; however, when the Marshal arrived at work the next day, the logs were still bound to the floating shack of George Chevrie. As Marshal Morris, a good and decent man by all testimonies, approached the home a few minutes later, the anger that was borne in the despondency of poverty overcame the river fisherman. He shot Marshal Morris in cold blood while the Marshal was stooping down with his pocket knife in hand to cut loose the only hope that the isolated man had left. In an instant, an innocent man was dead for the price of three or four logs.

It was only a few hours before the entire county had become outraged over the murder of their Marshal, especially at the hands of a degenerate river fisherman from Michigan. A horrible wrong had been done, and the justice afforded the law was too slow in its retribution for the likes of the mob. George Chevrie needed to be quickly dealt with so that true justice could be swiftly executed. As the night wore on and the drinking increased, the crowd gathered around the jailhouse holding Chevrie began chanting for a lynching. Mass hysteria grew among the revenge seekers of drunken men as someone in the mob commandeered a large wooden post deemed sufficient to stand as a battering ram for the jail door. The rebellious group quickly broke into the jailhouse, pushed aside Deputy John Kizer, whose resistance was negligible, grabbed the terrified perpetrator, and summarily and unapologetically marched him down to Marr Creek Bridge. They hung him from the metal rafters only a few feet from where I was standing. Another man participating in the melee was killed during the stampede on the jail, trampled to death in the confusion. George Chevrie hung there until the next afternoon. On the following Sunday, six men carried a box containing the body of Marshal John Morris, and placed him in his final resting place among the torment of his young wife and children. His funeral drew a deservedly large crowd. Many of the men at the funeral were the men at the lynching, comfortable in the justification of their righteous act. An eye for an eye. The people of Pocahontas took up a collection to ensure railroad passage for the widow Chevrie and her fatherless children to return to their native Michigan. It seemed the only Christian thing to do.

"Make you peace with God and ask him to forgive you for killing that Morris fella. You won't find forgiveness here." (Last words spoken to George Chevrie prior to his death at 1:30 a.m. in Pocahontas, Arkansas, March 23, 1901)

Leaving the riverside park, I walked a block over to Broadway Street, and then two blocks up to the Randolph County Courthouse. The grand concrete structure stood alone like a pillar of salt and looked like an overgrown mausoleum with its thick concrete columns and recessed entrance area. The county had erected a respectable War Memorial to those individuals who lost their lives serving in the defense of our great country. I thought of our son Aaron, who at the time was overseas in the Persian Gulf. Tears swelled in my eyes as I gazed across the bronze statues, but thinking only of my boy's face, and desperately wanting him back home. It was predominantly the sons and daughters from families in towns like this one that made

up the brave men and women of our Armed Services. My father served in Korea in the Navy, and now my son was following my father's path. The town proudly honored their service in a dignified and respectful manner, and I was impressed and grateful that such care was

Celebrated 1859 Meteor, proven not to be a meteor, Pocahontas, Arkansas town square

given to this effort by the people of Pocahontas. I stood alone, briefly closed my eyes, and said a prayer for my boy.

Almost adjacent to the memorial was the large stone that I had come to see, oddly secured by a short wrought iron black fence that I could have easily stepped over. Sitting alone on a large block of poured concrete, the mighty rock from the sky glistened against the afternoon sun in all of its historical and mythical glory. I marveled at the abundant stories that the old stone could probably tell, beginning far beyond our starry sky – or maybe not. Like so many things of mystery, its mythology exceeded its reality. Since the day it breached our atmosphere (or was dug up from beneath the ground as was the case in truth), the great rock had been hiding troves of celestial secrets inside of its hardened core. The rock of imperial distinction, despite all expert evidence to the contrary, bore an inscription carved unceremoniously across its topside that read, *"This METEOR Fell 1859. Donated by A. H. Keith."* The glorious bauble nicely decorated the Randolph County Courthouse lawn, amid mythological splendor, in the face of all doubters, proving again that people will believe what they want, irrespective of proof otherwise. Our best politicians relied heavily upon that human axiom, as did many of our best preachers.

I left the courthouse lawn and walked back toward the river and my truck. I could see the bridge ahead of me where George Chevrie lost his life to the rope. In an odd twist of fate and irony, Deputy John Kizer, the man responsible for protecting George Chevrie from the mob that night, but who offered little resistance as they rammed down the door of the jailhouse, would years later become the County Agriculture Agent and a part-time veterinarian, maintaining his home near Pocahontas. As people closest to Kizer dropped off dead like flies year after year, suspicions grew as to the source of the bad luck that accompanied many of those souls that knew him. Since the Chevrie lynching, Kizer had slowly worked his way into local prominence, responsible for assisting farmers with crop planting and harvesting and taking care of stock animals for his neighbors, although he had no such training. His loathing for dogs of all sorts, kinds, and breeds was widely known throughout the area. His common veterinarian solution for nearly any dog's ailment was to put the animal down with haste.

After skirting off years of suspicion, Kizer was eventually arrested for the mass killings of eleven people over three decades, apparently for life insurance payments from his victims. He was not prosecuted for his dog killings. His human victims included two wives, close friends and relatives, and his adopted son who died before his twentieth birthday. Kizer killed himself with strychnine poisoning hidden in his coat pocket in a syringe while being taken from the Paragould jail to Pocahontas for questioning regarding the murders. Along the trip, Kizer stated to the deputies in charge of his transfer that he feared being lynched by a mob of the town's citizens, like what had happened years earlier to George Chevrie. Many people of the community continued to doubt John Kizer's guilt. He had evidenced many of the deaths associated with his killings through sentimental monuments and memorials, although later found to have been purchased with life insurance proceeds of his victims. On the day of Kizer's death in 1936, the local squad car carrying his deceased body to the undertaker passed over the Mill Slough Bridge that had once held the lifeless body of river fisherman George Chevrie, the man given up to the mob while Deputy Kizer stood by and watched. The bridge's red paint by that time was badly fading but the beams of steel that held the weight of the hate remembered. The river fisherman finally had his revenge.

It was an unusual thing around the turn of the century for a white man like George Chevrie to be lynched. Normally, mob induced hangings in the two decades after the end of the Civil War were reserved for newly freed blacks, whose earned freedoms had released them to compete with whites for jobs and resources. These currents of racial infraction were felt in both northern and southern states, as evidenced by the brutal and unjustified hangings in Duluth, Minnesota in 1920 of three African American youth, a spectacle so grotesque that the town has now converted the location of the hangings into a memorial embracing diversification. The societal tensions resulting from the upheaval of the southern culture were catalysts to those individuals whose natures were evil by intent, or who were wholly unprepared to deal with the change in the system from which they had drawn such advantage for so long. Social change was perceived as threatening the old order, as was the case with change throughout the eons of time. Opportunity for one seemed always to threaten another. So often individual identity could be hidden beneath the veil of group consensus, a dark place where sin would fester like an open sore. Difference was to be feared and loathed, and institutions were to be hidden behind and within. The exclusion and removal of foreigners, as defined by the ruling class, would safeguard continued success of the existing, and so it went across the decades from one class or group to the next, until true change overran the obstructionism. At the time of the lynching of George Chevrie, religious piety was the primary basis of group identity and exclusionary hatred, and history really did repeat itself.

Ÿ

Chapter 12

« JUNCTION POINT »

The two small communities of Walnut Ridge and Hoxie folded right up on top of one another in an area of the state where not much else was left to notice; however, there may have never been two communities so far apart. In 1888, Hoxie emerged as an incorporated town due to the efforts of one woman, Mary A. Boas, who owned a sizable tract of land south of Walnut Ridge. As executives of the Kansas City, Springfield, and Memphis Railroad Corporation made the rounds in Walnut Ridge to secure easement lands for their track route and depot, they found much of the land overpriced, or not available due to residential small plot segmentation extending well away from Main Street, where they hoped to locate the depot. Speculators in the small town had caught railroad fever. Knowing that the track was on its way, many had purchased numerous parcels of land in anticipation of the most logical location for the path of the rail line. Noting the opportunity for her smaller community located just to the south, Mrs. Boas contacted railroad executives and pledged right-of-ways through her nearly five hundred acre tract as well as donated twenty acres upon which a depot could be constructed. The executives expeditiously accepted her proposal and the land speculators of Walnut Ridge were left holding an empty bag of opportunity lost. Not surprisingly, the first establishment in town was the twelve-room Boas Hotel, a frame structure built a block north of the newly constructed Hoxie Depot. If you followed the rail line out of Jonesboro along US#63, you could still see the southwestward bend that adjusted the line's angle from its original destination of Walnut Ridge south to Hoxie, where all the wise guys were left wondering how she did it to them.

The progressive thinking of Mary A. Boas began the tradition of this small community's embrace of opportunity and inevitable change. Sometimes big things can start from small places, and that was what happened in Hoxie; obscurity beginning what ended in amazement. Against all odds of logic and prediction, it was in Hoxie on June 25, 1955, that the School Superintendent, Kunkel Edward Vance, set forth a motion at the School Board meeting that summer to integrate the schools of Hoxie, and become the state's first fully integrated system. His decision for the recommendation was based on the ruling by the Supreme Court in May of the former year that all schools across the span of our country would eventually be fully integrated. Vance noted in later interviews regarding his thinking at the time that the integration plan was *"right in the sight of God, complied with the Supreme Court ruling, and was cheaper for the school system."* The subsequent vote of white school board members to integrate the small school system was unanimous, and the officials proceeded with plans to accomplish their goal before the new school year. Little controversy was anticipated, and no special preparations or fanfare were planned. Many school systems across the south were having the exact conversations regarding the future of their students and systems and how most appropriately to follow the new law; however, other school leaders were working equally as hard to find a way to ignore it, especially in Arkansas.

Nobody at the time could have cared about the plans of a small, rural school system in northern Arkansas who had few black students and no history of racial tensions. The black families of Hoxie frequently intermingled with their white neighbors in the course of their everyday lives; however, Hoxie was no integrated utopia. Like almost all of Arkansas in the mid-1950s, Hoxie's cultural and societal barriers set up boundaries for African Americans specifically designed not to be crossed. Eating establishments only served black patrons on a "to go" basis from the back of the local restaurants. The train depot, Hoxie's main community building and the pride of Mary Boas, had a small, segregated area for blacks, including separate restrooms and water fountain. There was not a hotel in Hoxie that would accommodate an African American for an overnight stay, and medical prescriptions had to be filled in Jonesboro at a black-owned pharmacy, since neither of the two local pharmacies in town would fill them.

It was an honorable notion to assume moral authority alone as the driving force behind the decision-making of the five white School Board members to vote for integration of their district during the summer of 1955, but the primary concern facing the School Board was budgetary in nature. Given the Supreme Court ruling of *Brown v. Board of Education of Topeka, Kansas*, the small community was faced with the added financial burden of busing the handful of high school aged African American students to nearby Booker T. Washington High School, a

segregated Negro high school located within the district but several miles east of Hoxie. Seeking additional support for their integration plan, Superintendent Vance approached the Walnut Ridge School Board to join them in their integration schedule. The recorded minutes from the Hoxie School Board meeting of July 25, 1955 reflected the response that Vance received from angry

1st School Day, Hoxie, Arkansas, July 25, 1955, from Life Magazine, "First Day of Integration"

members and individuals when he pitched them the idea in early July: *"No Action at Walnut Ridge."* Left to go it alone, the Hoxie Board moved forward with its plans.

Nobody really knows the exact connection point, but somehow *Life Magazine* became aware of the tiny town's intentions, and seeing an opportunity to highlight even the smallest of advances toward integration in the south, decided to run a series of innocuous photos of the first day of class in a pictorial review of its August 1955 edition. What the pictures showed the world were beautiful, kind, and innocent children from both races talking, playing, and learning without even a hint of discourse; a scene totally unacceptable and repugnant to the haters, who quickly organized in mass rejection of the implied equality as revealed in the article's photographs. The unprepared school board soon found itself at the center of incensed racial attention. Bigoted outside groups such as White America Inc., based in Pine Bluff, Arkansas, and the White Citizens' Council of Arkansas, based in Little Rock, descended upon the rural community, bringing with them a cloud of scorn and derision. Considerable political and community pressure was brought to bear against the original five members of the school board that had made the initial vote for integration, including a resolution with a thousand local signatures demanding the resignations of each of the four white Board members and Superintendent Vance's immediate termination without severance. It would be unfair not to recognize the tremendous strain and fear of retribution that these men lived under within the boundaries of the supposed security of their own homes. Violence to their person by some crazy zealot would have not been given a second thought. They were clearly men of purpose and courage despite the prevailing financial pragmatism.

"Therefore it is best for the two races to each have their separate existence. Racial mixing of children in schools will lead to undue familiarity and encourage intermarriage - a mongrel people." (Pastor Wesley Pruden, Broadmoor Baptist Church, Little Rock & President, Capital Citizens Council)

"God gave them (Negroes) talents to serve others; and there is no race that can compete with the Negro Race in this Field. The Negro is a lover of the outdoor life. The Negro will never speak or sing like the White Man, nor can the White Man speak or sing like the Negro." (Evangelist J. Harold Smith, *GOD's Plan for the Races: America's Number One Problem, Segregation*, University of Central Arkansas Archives and Special Collections)

Since a supposed emancipation, the African American race bore pain and assault against its collective character in Arkansas with brief intervals of peace, but no periods of real equality. The overriding politics in the 1950s, during the period that my father graduated from Little Rock Central High School about a mile from his downtown home, was dominated by southern Democrats who were staunchly and unashamedly segregationists to the core of their being. I have no idea to this day the basis of my father's family's experience with African Americans which would have set the baseline for their vile opinions, but the Hall family regrettably categorized all black people the same – as inherently inferior – as people to ignore and shun, or as people who should know their place and stay in it. The blacks most favored were the ones that accepted the status quo and kept quiet about any need for change. When I was a child, growing up among my aunts and uncles on that side of the family, the word *"Nigger"* was tossed about in conversation without a hint of embarrassment or shame. There was little differentiation among black people from their perspective, except to segregate them into further derogatory groups through indecent slang and characteristic reference. The purpose of the demeaning language was to reduce African Americans into childlike categories, therefore requiring parental oversight from whites. Persons of color were expected to address whites with due respect, such as greeting my parents as *"Mr. or Mrs. Hall,* while the whites were conditioned to return the kindness using only the first name of the African American. *"Good morning, Mrs. Hall!"* *"Good morning, Thomas."* I never thought a thing about this when I was a boy. It was just what was done, or at least, it was just what was done by our family in large measure. Overriding the language was a structural value system rooted in pure racism that supported the erroneous belief that despite my family's poverty, they were more deserving of success; despite their lack of formal education, they were inherently smarter; despite their meager social status, they were more culturally astute; and despite their shared faith in God, they had claim to more divine favor.

My extended family's deep belief in the righteousness of segregation seemed to have no real footing in personal experience, but was widely encouraged and supported through southern institutionalized discrimination, a kind of *"this is the way things are supposed to be."* My paternal family's negative views of black people appeared to be rooted more in a lack of direct experience than through direct experience. They were afraid, not of what they knew, but what they did not know; and more importantly, who they did not know. It was a hard thing to view in retrospect my loving and gentle grandparents, and aunt and uncle, as racist. Both people were kind, giving, and charitable, within the scope of their self-imposed societal boundaries. I do not believe that my grandparents would have withheld anything from me that I needed for which they were capable of giving; however, the insensitivity of their language and the warped perspective of their defined worldview, supported an unequal societal structure, implicitly accepted as divine order.

When I was a teenager visiting my grandmother, a kind and considerate black man stopped along the sidewalk in front of my grandmother's porch. The neighborhood by now was more plural than in earlier years, as African Americans migrated into the homes left vacant near downtown Little Rock. Tipping his tattered Bowler hat in respectful acknowledgement toward my grandmother, he said, *"Good morning, Mrs. Hall,"* she returning his friendly greeting as they exchanged a brief moment of small talk. These two people were, after all, neighbors, and seemed to enjoy each other's company. As the gentleman made his way up the sidewalk and out of our earshot, my grandmother turned to me, and I will never forget what she said. *"That's Mr. Anderson. He's the nicest nigger man you'd ever want to meet."* Such an example encapsulated the dichotomy of sins of omission versus sins of commission to me; yet, sins nonetheless. Unrecognized insensitivity from people just like my father's family, blind to their own deeply rooted prejudice, was fuel to the fire of the race haters, who promoted a predominantly bigoted southern society secured by Godly decree. The markers set to that baseline continue to hem in our world.

While the years softened my parent's rhetoric, their structural beliefs – those found at the core of how they actually viewed the world – changed little toward African Americans, or anyone different for the most part; the "others". When not forced to think, they were free to remain blinded from the extraordinary benefits of the structural preferential treatment afforded whites across all social spectrums; quality of education, access to capital, and political influence, just to name a starter group. Among their social peers, our suburban neighbors, and the fellow members of the Moose Lodge, there was an aversion toward the advancement and achievement of African Americans. Blacks were not welcomed upon the stage of opportunity inside the circles of my parents influence. My mother and father were affronted by the vocal arguments and demonstrations set forth by assertive black leaders that equality was their unassailable right. They believed that black people were and deserved to be, by default, second class citizens. For a large portion of my youth, I listened to my parents and relatives of the Hall family denounce Civil Rights leaders, mock the suffering of African Americans as self-inflicted, and flee from every opportunity to expose themselves, and their children, to a richer diversity and a more Christ-like humanity.

When the trouble started at Little Rock Central High School in 1957, my parents packed up and moved from their downtown Little Rock home and followed the wave of white flight across the river into North Little Rock. When my father was transferred to Memphis in 1967, we settled instead in predominantly white (at the time) West Memphis, as there was black trouble brewing in Memphis, which culminated a year later in the sanitation strike and the participative march of Dr. Martin Luther King. During the summer of 1968, my father was given charge of opening a new sales territory east of the Shelby County line, stretching up to near Nashville. Jackson, Tennessee was the geographical center of that new territory and the obvious choice for a new hometown. Instead, our family moved to the smaller Brownsville during the summer of 1968, the town which served as the headquarters of the Tennessee Klan. It was in this small community that my father was recruited to attend what was communicated to him to be a civic men's meeting, which turned out to be a Klan meeting. He did not attend future meetings, but the fact that he was invited at all reflected a viewpoint, a commonality, that he shared with many of those who did. Our family finally moved two years later to Jackson, but only because my parent's marriage had been so damaged while in Brownsville that they believed, rightly so in retrospect, that a new place would also mean a new start. In Jackson, we settled in the north side of Madison County, outside of the city limits. African Americans made up the majority of citizens inside of the city limits on the south side of town.

Before we left Brownsville, my experiences there taught me some of my own lessons from the town folk about white supremacy. The dry cleaners, for example, located near the town square, had a large sign displayed in its front window that read, *"No Coloreds."* The first time I noticed this sign as a fourth grader, I remember asking my Dad if that meant that they only took white clothes. In those days, the town maintained a public swimming pool within the boundaries of the small city park. I never saw a black child swimming in the pool, except for one day when three black teenagers, young men probably around the ages of fifteen to seventeen, showed up at the pool and gathered around one of the side tables, undressing into their swim trunks. The response from the horrified mothers sitting around the pool was as you would expect. As soon as it became apparent that the young men fully intended to swim among the white children in the public pool, mothers began jerking their kids out of the pool in haste. I climbed out with all of the other white kids and stood around the pool watching in amazement, like we were looking at mystical creatures. The boys, undeterred, eased themselves into the pool, and began taking dives and doing cannonballs. I remember the look in their eyes. It was hurtful, but they were likewise determined. One mother went over to the edge of the pool, which was now completely void of anyone except the three black youth, and spat in it. Others followed, and people began shouting obscenities at the young men. Some of the older white boys huddled up in a corner as if planning a reprisal. Inside of five minutes, the African American youth having made their point, slowly and methodically climbed out of the pool, redressed, and left the area. Many of the mothers and children followed them into the parking lot, unwilling, I assumed, to reenter the swimming pool after them deeming it tainted by the black skin of the youths. By the time the local police showed up at the pool, the young men had disappeared across the train tracks that demarcated the color line of the town.

In Brownsville, my father and I would often fish in backwater ponds that lined the Hatchie River bottom a few miles south of town. I cherished these times with my Dad more than any other activity. Basically, the area was a swamp, and on many occasions we saw large water moccasins that put our attention on notice of the dangers of these particular spots; however, the fishing in these overflow ponds could be extremely rewarding, so we pressed on. We fished for anything that would bite a rubber worm and rarely threw anything back. Our technique in the muddy water was to hurl a sinker-laden rubber worm as far as we could from the bank, allowing it to settle along the bottom of the pond, and then slowing retrieve it. The strikes would normally come from larger fish, lazily sitting along the bottom at the same time that our worm bumped across his path. On this particular day, I snagged what felt like a whale, and nearly backed up fifty feet from the shore into the woods in my haste to retrieve it onto the bank.

When the mighty fish was finally beached, I ran over to have a look at my prize. To my horror, there was not a trophy bass lying among the brush, but rather, a lowly five pound carp. My father came running and arrived just in time to see the big fish lying on the ground. I looked up at him and said, *"It's a nigger fish, Dad,"* using a common term of identification for that species that I had heard my Uncle Ralph use on many occasions. The moment the words came out of my mouth, I remember a sinking feeling entering my soul, as if a piece of me was pulled out that could never be replaced. Despite all of my exposure of being taught how to loathe black people, up to that point, I had never spoken that word. My father patted me on the back and told me what a nice job I had done landing it. He unhooked the large carp, ran a piece of string tied to a stick through its gills, and carried it around to the other side of the pond, a good distance from where I was fishing. I saw him hold the fish up for examination in front of an old black man that was fishing across the way with a cane pole. The old black man reached for my fish and took hold of it with nodding approval. On our way back home that afternoon, I asked my father why the black man liked to eat carp, but we didn't. He told me that carp were a particularly boney fish, and hard to eat, as it took a lot of effort to piece through and past hundreds of tiny bones to get at the meat. *"Black people don't seem to mind the bones as much as us whites,"* he told me. *"I guess they're used to the extra work."*

UNITED KLANS OF AMERICA, INC.
Realm of Tennessee, Brownsville, Tennessee 38012

"From the Resolutions make(made) by the United Klans of America: To re-dedicate ourselves to the great principles which define Americanism involving Christian Tradition, Racial Self Respect, Private Enterprise, Constitutional Government, the Sovereignty of the individual, the Local Gobernment(Government) Unit and the Government of the United States.

Some of us have been asleep for too long. We have let the enemies of our great coutry(country) sneak into the main stream of our national life. One by one they have belittled and diminished in our minds the principle upon which America was founded and the laws laid mercifully down for us by our founding fathers.

First and formost(foremost) of these traditions given to us is the cornerstone of our nation which is Christ and the Christian ideals. We must realize that the enemies of Christ are the enemies of America for upon this main ideal we were founded. Without the Christian tenets of faith to sustain us there will be no America.

Next we all feel and believe that our race of people, the white race is truly our only heritage. Every effort must be made to stop the Mongrelizers from forcing us to become all one color. The pure white race has done more spiritually and physically to aid progress with the help of God than any other race of people in the world.

(Rhodes College, *Crossroads to Freedom*, 2008-04-05, resolution archive of Brownsville, Tennessee meeting of the United Klans of America, Inc.)

The cultural environment of my youth saw a world where every person was created equal, but not created for equal opportunity. To my knowledge, no person in my family ever participated in a segregationists meeting or demonstration, nor did they ever invoke violence upon any African American. The inadvertent attending of a KKK meeting by my Dad on one occasion invoked no interest in his returning. "I'm not in love with the blacks," he said, "but I'm not interested in stirring up a bunch of trouble, either." It was the Hall family's language and world view, joined with complacency, which engendered its own kind of attack against equality. My family's tacit acceptance of racism unabated, when bundled with thousands of others likewise conceded, created a garden where intolerance could fruitfully seed, and it blinded their eyes to the unending disparity of civil treatment and withheld opportunity that was the daily experience of southern African Americans. That was where my Hall family ultimately failed humanity and why even today I still bear some of its shame. By embracing the status quo of the time, my family took little intentioned action to make life worse for African Americans, and we took no action whatsoever to make it any better. I was grateful that I witnessed my father change his language and his heart before his death in 1983, but too late in his life for any recompense, except regret.

My personal early experiences of racial antagonism from Little Rock, West Memphis, to Brownsville, mirrored a vile period of abuse toward minorities across the south, widely documented through their continued struggles for equal treatment, equal expectation, and equal value. In 1957, the same year that I was born at Baptist Hospital in Little Rock, the Governor of the state forbade nine African American high school students from entering Little Rock Central High School. The National Guard was called out to protect the "Little Rock Nine." The white population was stirred into constant hysteria with the hateful rhetoric spewing from the mouths of expedient politicians and ignorant church pastors who tried to hide their own repulsive beliefs behind perverse interpretations of God's Word. The most contemptible rumor alleged by the radical segregationists centered on the implied causal black movement being motivated by African American men desiring to get into the beds of white women. This storyline was the standard rhetoric used to fuel the flames of aversion.

The Dyer Anti-lynching Bill, initially introduced to Congress in 1918, was effectively stalled for fifty years by the bigoted white Democrats that comprised the southern states' U. S. Senatorial electorate. Always under the guise of protecting the hordes of white women that could find themselves victims of the ravenous sexual advances of black men, the white segregationists constantly voiced the fear of unabated male African American sexual aggression in justification of their own self-serving debauchery. One of the Dyer Bill's strongest opponents was Thaddeus Caraway, the transplanted Arkansas U.S. Senator from Jonesboro, who consistently characterize the Dyer Bill as *"a bill to encourage rape"* of white women by dark skinned men. Thaddeus Caraway had commented that NAACP support of the Dyer Bill intended *"to make rape permissible, and to allow the guilty to go unpunished if that rape should be committed by a Negro on a white woman in the South."* The Daughters of the American Revolution, on this topic, took no commemorative action regarding his position.

In more modern times, a young man from the same city of Jonesboro entered into the living room of psychiatric patient

Leland Irby to conduct his normal weekly review of his physical, medical, and emotional status. Bill Penix, Jr. survived his tour in Vietnam, and spent several years struggling with the mental effects of the war, residual efforts that he attributed to his years of living with alcoholism. Having overcome these sizable obstacles, the dedicated veteran became a mental health professional, working in and around his hometown of Jonesboro, determined to serve in a capacity that helped people. He cared for patients in their own homes and made weekly rounds in support of their well-being. As Penix was attempting to draw blood from Irby, without provocation, his patient pulled a hunting knife from his pocket and stabbed the young healthcare worker twenty times with a serrated blade on the morning of March 27, 1991, around 9:00 a.m. Bill Penix, Jr. died before the ambulance arrived. The mother of the victim, Marian Penix, was a well-respected attorney in town, later serving as a District Judge. Her distinguished career included being the first woman on the Arkansas State Court of Appeals, appointed by Governor Bill Clinton in 1979. She followed her son in death later that year in September. Bill Penix, Sr., himself a renowned attorney in Jonesboro, said of his wife, *"She was just a magnificent woman. My wife has been my conscience all of my life."*

One such time of conscience was in 1955 in Hoxie, Arkansas, not many years after Bill Penix, Sr. started his fledgling law practice with his wife Marian. While other attorneys fervently avoided the controversy, Penix and Penix agreed to represent the Hoxie School Board in a lawsuit filed against them by radical segregationist Herbert Brewer, the Hoxie Citizens' Committee, attorney Amis Guthridge, White America, Inc., Jim Johnson, Curt Copeland and the White Citizens' Council of Arkansas, requesting a restraining order to stop further integration interference of its school system. Bill Penix, Sr. argued successfully to the courts that *"Vance and the School Board had a duty to desegregate the district following the Brown v. Board decision."* The Hoxie School Board prevailed in District Court, setting an example for the rest of the country as to what was to come, and benchmarking the civic struggle that it would take to get there. Following the court victory, Superintendent K. E. Vance resigned his position and left the area in fear for his family's safety. The Attorney General of Georgia, concerned with the broad impact upon his state of a ruling from a Federal District Court in favor of school segregation, filed a brief under leave of the court as *amicus curiae*, opposing the courts favorable ruling.

In fact, even in Hoxie, it took more than moral motivation to move the mountain of segregation that stood in its path. It took legal compulsion and the threat of losing federal education dollars in their state's budgets. This was government actually serving its purpose. With hearts bent on hate and inequality, laws could be used to compel justice. Had the school board not been led at that time by the progressive K. E. Vance, and if they had been supported with a stronger financial budget which would have financed the required busing expenditures, nobody would have ever heard of Hoxie, Arkansas.

The character of those school board members still deserved recognition, as irrespective of the original motivating factors, they held their ground while being confronted with the most heinous form of opposition. After things settled down in Hoxie, and life returned to the monotony of farming and storekeeping, the black children, now fully integrated into the school system, remained mostly isolated from the participative activities and dignities afforded their white peers. Unlike the first day of school, when the innocence of youth attached them to one another's curiosity, they witnessed in the actions of their grownup parents how to enforce a separation of prejudice. As always, there were one or two real champions in and among the small contingency opposing the mass of rabble-rousers, with K. E. Vance, and the husband-wife attorney team of Bill and Marian Penix, counted among the most courageous. True to his family's long-held convictions against the death penalty, Bill Penix, Sr. remained steadfast to his values in the face of personal tragedy. As Leyland Irby was being prosecuted for the murder of his son, Bill Penix, Sr. solicited mercy from the courts on behalf of the deranged man not to impose an execution, stating to the public that he did not desire to have a second senseless death follow his son's senseless death. There were always people willing to jump onto the backs of the brave and exploit the moral high ground when the time to do so was conveniently safe from the risks that burdened the truly courageous. Courage was rarely required during convenient times, which accounted for why we should admire it when demonstrated by the best of us.

I filled up my truck at T-Ricks Citgo at the south side of Hoxie, followed the rail tracks another mile south, and headed east toward Jonesboro. Darkness was overtaking the plowed fields of chopped cotton. As the top quarter of the big yellow ball fell over the edge of the brown earth behind me, thin pink and gray lines streaked the sky against the setting sun in my rear view mirror. I pondered this magnificence and thought of Pam. She had always kept me looking at the potential of people rather than at the obvious. At that moment, my soul ached to be with her and to gaze upon her inward and outward beauty, realizing just how conscious I was in that moment that she had been my conscience all of my life, too.

White River, Oil Trough, Arkansas

Chapter 13

« WHITE RIVER »

I just made the city limits of Jonesboro as darkness settled in for the night. Still outside of town, I noticed a brightened area off in the distance that I instantly recognized as the lights of a high school football field. Friday night high school football was the one thing that transcended the generations, religion, ethnicity, and cultural differences across the entire south. The high school gridiron was the highest per square foot of color blind piece of southern geography one could find, where locals made their final athletic stand and clung to stories of lore far beyond their expiration date. In that exchange of experience between fathers and sons, and mothers and daughters, the glories of the previous generation became the base of expectation of the next, and so on, and so on. Small town life could leave a person stuck in those years, especially if they enjoyed the security of consistency. The ensuing legacy of high school bravado falsely empowered the fragile egos of those people who in adult life would achieve little else, leaving the rest of us forced to relive the tales of youthful exploits, trying our best to ignore the reality of their commonplace present. Had I failed to mention that I hit .374 my senior year and led our division in doubles, and that my American Legion team went to the state finals that same year? Parting company with glory of any size was a sorrow's end.

Upon arriving at the Holiday Inn Express south of town, a kind and perky young lady with a northern accent checked me in, explaining that complimentary breakfast began at 6:00 a.m. and that the password to the Internet was written inside of the key jacket. She wore a large red silk rose pinned into the back bun of her dark hair, as if determined to hang onto the last vestige of warm days before the soon onset of winter. I asked her how she came into central Arkansas from her obviously northern roots, and she replied that she came to the area to study music and get away from the harsh winters of the north. She wanted to be near family, if possible, and had an aunt who was a school teacher in the city. She liked the south most in the winters and dreaded it most in the summers, which led me to smile and concur. Bidding the young lady a good night, I headed up to the room, and after quickly checking in with Pam, fell into the bed, drifting off to sleep and wondering about tomorrow.

I chased sleep throughout the night, but never caught it. The strange bed and noises kept me tossing and turning, nodding in and out, and twisting my bed covers into a pile. I was still stirring before the first rays of light sifted through the drawn, thick curtains of the hotel window. Remaining in that beautiful *in-between* space of unconsciousness and looming consciousness, I lay still and quiet, slowly gaining awareness of the early morning sounds of the new day. Sporadic hums of traffic passed by outside of my window, each type of vehicle pitching high in its coming and humming low in its going. The large diesel trucks had the most distinctive voice, rolling by the hotel like great frogs bellowing in announcement of the coming day. I started thinking about the road ahead and the road behind, things seen and yet unseen, not quickly willing to acknowledge my present reality.

Too often, upon immediately waking, I allowed the thoughts of immediacy to cover over time for reflection. It was the beginning of my third day on this pilgrimage of my southern ancestry. I was seeing a lot and learning a lot. The long travel days provided me ample time for thinking and reflecting and sorting, without feeling the self-imposed pressure of immediate understanding and application. I was free to let my thoughts move as a lava lamp, free to float around and bump into one another and free to join and unjoin as desired. This method was contrary to my usual approach, burdened with a brain which worked in systematic analysis, normally slicing and dicing the data from which to draw a logical conclusion. Perhaps, the greatest gift of this trip was the time alone and the clarity of noticing that the person I thought about the most was also the person that waited for me back home. The pain of the past would have to stay there, and I prayed that it would. Our marriage had endured more heartache than many, less than some, and we had loved deeply and hurt deeply. There were no longer children in the home to take our attention away from one another or to use as an excuse to push things aside that needed discussion. It was just us again, like when we started, but all of the ideals of youth had long since receded into the realities of age, and now in advanced midlife, I so wanted us to finish well, and finish well together. At that thought, I started wishing for home.

After showering, I wandered down to the lobby to enjoy the promised complimentary breakfast and juice and took a table to myself in the small café area to review my e-mails and finish my coffee. The television was tuned to Fox News so it quickly diverted my attention to my I-Pad to check e-mail. I grabbed a small glass of orange juice from the push-button dispensary unit, and returning to the table, leafed through a copy of the local paper, the *Jonesboro Sun*, which a hotel patron had evidently discarded. It was a couple of days old but provided me something to look at instead of the television. Scanning over the articles of local interests brought a smile to my face and a reminder of the truthful adage that *"all politics are local."* The small town paper covered everything from the national election that was forthcoming to the personal obituaries of its newly deceased citizens. In the *"Hometown"* section of the paper, among the news of the week was that Central Baptist Church, now located in a sprawling campus near the south loop, was supporting evacuees of Hurricane Ike in their outreach efforts. The article continued that these souls were mostly folks from Louisiana, who had also endured the pain of earlier Hurricane Gustav. Since the devastation of Katrina, the Mississippi, Louisiana, and Alabama coast had been consistently battered from the adverse weather coming off of the Gulf of Mexico, and in the opinion of most climate scientists, we were in for more of it in the years to come. I traveled to the Alabama coast and the Florida panhandle a full year after the storm wrecked the area, and the devastation was still wide and pronounced. It was hard to get a clear feeling from television as to the extent of the devastation and the associated heartache. In that case, a picture did not tell a thousand words. It was harder still to see it in person.

Some of the families receiving assistance from the church in Jonesboro were no doubt still trying to recover from Katrina and were faced now with yet another wave of catastrophe. Like the constant beating of ocean waves, life was sometimes that way. The newspaper highlighted the depth of assistance and merit worthiness of the work that the local body of believers committed to the cause of helping disadvantaged families through these hard times. The news story instantly recalled to my mind how Kurt, himself a dedicated Southern Baptist at the time, had joined a group of men headed straight into the horrors of the aftermath of Hurricane Katrina, shovels, chain saws, and determination in hand. For months on end after the disaster, his group of caring responders literally worked night and day, all volunteered assistance, through several trips and extensive fundraising efforts, to rebuild the home of a family that before the storm enjoyed a nice ranch home filled with a lifetime of memories. That good work by my friend and that group of men was an example of the best that church could be, because church was always better when looking outside of their own walls to find purpose rather than when looking inside to find like-mindedness.

I could reference my own experience with the evangelical church, and fully understood the thin line between Godly obedience and misdirected self-indulgence, where evil would slither in quietly and unnoticed with incremental advancement, like ivy growing on old rocks. Central Baptist Church, the kind people about whom I was reading, struggled from the onset with the nature of human frailty, being the principle body of believers involved in the Jonesboro Church Wars of the 1930s, where factions were formed around charismatic personalities more than piety, and the battle against the flesh was taken up with guns rather than Bibles. The Christian life could not be obtained in zealotry, no matter how dedicated in its pursuit, but the constitution of Christ was found in humility, a rejection of our will to that of others. Forgiveness was the test of true faith, as our sins rarely pounced upon us like lions, but rather, we invited them in, like a mysterious stranger, initially intrigued by their allure, and then eventually overcome by their ruin. Sin was a slow burning ember, unless constantly guarded against and then quickly extinguished upon notice, its flames would spread to engulf your treasure and burn down what you held most dear. When the fire caught, the damage could quickly spread, as was my experience. There was a time, maybe in a dream, or on a day, when I watched while love faded before my eyes, and the bees began to die without my notice, and in what seemed like only an instant, I was searching for my heart among the ashes and dirt. That was what I knew of my walk with God - an experience of fire and wind and water.

"We have learned a bit too late in the day that action springs not from thought but from a readiness for responsibility." (Dietrich Bonhoeffer, *Letters and Papers from Prison*, as quoted in *Bonhoeffer: Pastor, Martyr, Prophet, Spy*, Eric Metaxas)

It was cloudy outside with an obvious threat of rain, as a cold front was certainly headed this way. I checked in with the hotel staff to get a printout of my bill and hustled back up to the room to pack and then hit the road. Just outside of town I passed the Westside Middle School and was shaken to recall the horrific events that took place there a decade ago. During the mid-1990s, a local boy of a single mother named Mitchell Scott Johnson periodically attended Sunday school at Central Baptist Church of Jonesboro, where he sang in the youth choir among his peers. A few years later, the now remarried mother of two, moved her membership to the Revival Tabernacle Church on the west side of town, near the small community of Bono. Notwithstanding the sincere efforts of the boy's mother to provide him a basis in faith, young Johnson did not take to heart the message of love, and patience, and peace. Other factors pulled strongly at his darker consciousness. He built a reputation among his classmates as that of being a loner, and wasn't that what was always said about boys who went wrong. Others called him a bully. What demons filled this young man's mind would never be known, and if known, never understood.

Infatuated with guns even at his early age, Johnson became familiar with the effective usage of weapons, and their permanent effects upon the targets of their aim. He was taught as a child that much of his identity was tied up in a relationship with a weapon. Perhaps motivated by the shunning of his advances from a young female classmate, or because of the encouragement of his younger cousin Andrew Golden, Johnson joined Golden on March 24, 1998 in the woods near their school in a shooting rampage that killed four young female students and a female teacher. An additional nine students and one teacher were injured. The young Golden pulled the fire alarm to the school's security system, and then the two boys shot indiscriminately into the fleeing crowd from a hidden position in the nearby woods. They were both apprehended by local police before fleeing the scene. Widely known as the *Jonesboro School Killings*, Arkansas law in 1998 only remanded the two serial killers to prison sentencing until their 21st birthday, whereupon both of their criminal records were expunged, and they were released from prison as free men. Johnson at the time of the shootings was 13 years old. Golden was 11 years old. A picture on the cover of the April 6th, 1998 edition of *Time*

Magazine entitled, *"Armed and Dangerous,"* of a baby Andrew Golden holding a rifle, forever memorialized the contempt that many gun restriction supporters felt toward families that grew up with guns and viewed them as essential assets of their lives. On the other side of the argument were the gun owners, the majority of people across this state, and many states, with whom there resided an unwavering commitment to keep anything remotely classified as a firearm free of any restriction. Five families still lived in this community with the daily pain of those horrible actions perpetrated by horribly misguided young men, and I could not begin to understand the depth of sorrow that would accompany burying a child killed in violence. No sane person wanted children to die from a weapon used by a crazy person, and no sane person believed that government could effectively stop deaths from occurring when evil was insistent upon action. Despite the hazy sky and all of the things that I did not understand, and other things without real answers, in this moment of fog and misty rain, I was left only to delight in my life and be grateful for it, for the protection that had blessed our children, and seeing ever so clearly how one life impacts another, through good or evil, and extends consequences farther than we can imagine.

The mountains held many dreams that I had chosen to remember from my youth: the rustle of the windblown autumn leaves on the dry ground, the crispness of the morning air against my face, the way the rocks bulged from beneath the thin soil to expose their backs and broken faces, the smell of burning wood from round stone chimneys, the faint echo of creaking limbs in groves of tall timbers, the sight of twisted shadows struggling against the light through the creek-carved hollows and narrows, silvery water running over and around limestone boulders piled up on one another like marbles, and bubbling and popping sounds of mountain streams flowing toward crystal lakes where fish lay ready to rise to my lure. Each experience singularly folded into a kaleidoscope of memory, playing through my mind in a grand symphony of sensory experience and emptied of the human frailty that so frequently embroiled my life. Nature was again filling my soul with boldness and delight. Across this wide plateau and beneath the stately white oaks, lay the remnants of my family's history, stories, truths, and regrets that I hoped to follow them into, and in so doing, build my own history for others to follow, and find home again. I caught a quick glimpse of a long string of Mallards just before disappearing from my view into gray fog. They looked to be headed almost due west, framed in the familiar V-pattern of their flight. I pulled quickly to the side of the road and stepped up onto the side rail of my pickup, straining my eyes to see them melt into the overcast sky. By now they were flying over the Cache River or Village Creek. I bet they had the swamp flats of the Black River in sight, and I was fast on their trail.

Peel Road, Jamestown Mountain, Batesville

Chapter 14

« PEEL FERRY »

The land along Highway 14 into south Batesville was flatter than I remembered. The leaves were changing colors on the back side of their fall patterns, so the trees carried a lot of brown in their foliage. At Locust Grove, the Jamestown Mountain came into clear view, its wide girth framing the southern arch of high ridges that protected the Batesville valley from the indiscriminate winds which terrorized Arkansas during the tornado season. It was around this hilltop that the Peel family set down roots for a few years.

"In 1814 a colony from Kentucky settled near Batesville, at the Greenbrier settlement. In 1815 further immigration to this place increased its population to nineteen families. The descendants of these families have been represented in the state by a Congressman, Samuel W. Peel, a Governor, W. R. Miller, and by many other officers." (The History of Arkansas: A Text-book for Public Schools, Josiah Hazen Shinn, 1905)

By the time of my grandparents' birth just before the turn of the 20th century, our Peels had settled broadly into north central Arkansas, joined a generation later by the Blairs who migrated from Carroll County in west Tennessee. Both families established homes and farms between Cove Creek at the northern boundary and Lower Cadron Creek at the south and east. The number of times they left the state of Arkansas could be counted on one hand, living long and full lives for the most part in a way not understood in our more modern world. It was a level of *just getting by* that I had never known and was taught not to expect or accept. Things they needed, but could not find locally to buy or barter, they made. Things they needed, but could not afford to make, trade, or buy, they did without. A thick Sears Catalog that sat around their clapboard house was the sole source of exposure to any items of luxury. From the catalog, my grandmother, Ruth, purchased bolts of cloth and boxes of needles to be put to the work of her strong hands and the rhythm of her foot-peddle sewing machine. Most of the time, they improvised with what was available.

Oscar Allen and Ruth Blair Peel, circa 1910

For instance, the toilet paper inside of the two-hole outhouse that sat at the rear of my grandparent's property, at my first memory of it, was held by an old mirror bracket that Papa found in a junk pile somewhere along the road. He put it to use by bolting it onto the plank wall at a serviceable angle to hold the roll. There were many other such examples of exemplary country engineering. As a child I drew water from their well into a long metal cistern tied to a rope pulley which was fashioned to the cross beam of the tin roofed shed that was constructed over the well opening. As the metal tube was lowered into the well, I listened for the distinct sound of the last air bubble leaving its place inside the tube, signaling that it was filled and ready to be pulled to the surface. Once above ground, I pulled a trigger on the back of the cistern tube to release the water into an enamel bucket which served to supply water needs for cleaning and cooking.

My grandmother Ruth and I often dug potatoes with a Maddox blade and standard hoe, and plowed the weeds from the garden with a push-wheel single blade plow that was navigated by two curved wooden handles in conjunction with considerable human effort. It was a lifestyle that would be ridiculed by young people today, certainly unimaginable by the standards of my own children. My recollections of the outhouse experiences alone, especially during the hottest of the summer days of Arkansas, swatting the flies while holding my nose, was enough to make me shutter even now. Despite all of their readily apparent poverty, my grandfather kept a beautiful 12HP Sears's riding mower and tow-along trailer that the grandchildren simply loved to drive, ride, and use with without restriction. They could not afford a flush toilet, and drew all of their water from an open well, but they could afford a riding tractor. Go figure. He always had new decks of playing cards, too. Among the abundance of unexplainable things about humans was that we make up our minds on what we must have and what we can live without, and for Oscar Peel, playing cards was a must have, and indoor plumbing was something he could live without.

I circled around the mountain on Jamestown Loop, but arrived near the top on the eastern side, only to find that access to Peel Road blocked with a set of concrete poles connected by a steel cable. The reason behind blocking passage to this side of Peel Road was unknown, but there was nobody to complain to, so I retraced my path back down the mountain and circled around to the western access point along Heber Springs Road. On my way up the ridge, I passed a large radio tower, followed by a couple of dilapidated homes that looked as though they had been first set to foundation a hundred years ago. I jumped out and took a quick photo, wondering about their history or if that family knew my family. I don't know what I expected from my visit, but my arrival was almost inconsequential in its normality. No bolts of lightning. No particularly interesting geographic formations. The only object of any consequence was the dated fire tower located at the pinnacle of the mountain, which I considered climbing for a brief moment before excusing that thought to wiser counsel.

After standing for several minutes examining the horizon and waiting for inspiration, but finding none, I returned to the inside of my truck cab and drove down the mountain, away from Peel Road and made my way back to Highway 14. Stopping in for gasoline at Almond's only store, I filled up my tank and purchased a soda along with a fine jar of Arkansas Raw Honey, packaged by Tim Roth of Altheimer, Arkansas. I turned my truck northwest toward some of the most beautiful country that God ever carved from rock, the Buffalo River gorge. I decided that the extra time to stay the course with Highway 14 would be well worth the effort, as it would eventually spit me out just south of my ending destination at Peel Ferry. The only caveat was that I had to make Peel Ferry before 6:30 p.m., or close to that, or it was going to be a long drive around the lake in the dark to reach Theodosia.

About an hour later, I pulled into the mountain retirement community of Mountain View where my Aunt Hetty lived for over forty years. It had been half that long since I visited her here, and while the town looked like it did the last time I saw it, I certainly did not. After circling the general area for a couple of blocks, I found Clarence Street and followed it west until spotting her small home on the right. I knocked on the door, simultaneously shouting, *"Aunt Hetty? It's Kenny. It's your nephew. Are you home?"* I heard her rustling around for a few seconds inside of the home, and then the door swung open, revealing my aging aunt in her wheel chair, all smiles as always, arms outstretched for a hug. *"My goodness, Kenny. How much you look like Daddy."*

After sitting for a few minutes and catching up on the years of separation, Aunt Hetty started talking about our larger family, cousins and children and grandchildren, about where they lived and how they were doing and what they did for a living. I had not been a faithful attendee of the annual reunion at Woolly Hollow and was admonished by Aunt Hetty for same. In her characteristic happy enthusiasm, she grabbed one of three or four remotes that were sitting on a side table near the couch, pointed it at the television and accessory equipment stacked beneath the television stand, and clicked through a list of saved videos which she detailed to me, explaining each scene as to characters in the frame and relationships to our family. At the end of a good thirty minutes of video, I mentioned that I needed to get back on the road to catch the ferry before dusk. As I was saying my goodbyes, she asked me to pull out a green folder that was squeezed upright between rows of books, and hand it to her. She looked up at me with the eyes of a teenager, *"You recognize this, don't you?"* Indeed, I did recognize the binder as my grandmother's *Book of Memories* that had been prepared in her honor after her death by my cousin. *"Let me read you a couple of these before you leave."* Implored by my aged aunt, I nodded and sat down onto the edge of the sofa.

Aunt Hetty flipped through the slightly worn pages of the notebook, her eyes peering across the words in standard typeface, *A Little Sense and Nonsense from Days Gone By – Ruth Peel.* I knew that inside there were hundreds of quips, poems, stories, and yarns that Granny Peel recited from memory during her lifetime. There was not a person that knew my simple grandmother that would believe for an instant that she was simple-minded. Instead, it was known across the reach of my family the breadth and depth of Ruth Peel's intelligence and cognitive abilities. Being poor did not equate to unschooled. Hetty read: *"A wise head holds a still tongue."* Turning a page or two, *"If you can't be a star in the sky, be a candle where you are."* Then, *"Show me the way not to fortune and fame, not how to win laurels or praise for my name, but show me the way to spread the "great story" that Thine is the Kingdom and Power and Glory."*

Upon hearing that poem, I was deeply moved, particularly given the grace and beauty of their voicing by my aunt, still exuding confidence and optimism for life, despite her proximity to the end of hers. I wondered, watching her read from the binder holding the memories of her mother in her wrinkled hands, if I would have the same level of dignity and grace as age overcame my own life. A life as long lived as Aunt Hetty's life included its share of heartbreak, and I was encouraged by the thought that the bitterness that still periodically circled through me could in time be forgotten, and that I could find forgiveness in the asking and in the giving. Age gave us the time we needed to set things right with ourselves, with others, and with God. She read:

"Great is the power of might and mind, but only Love can make us kind, and all we are or hope to be, is empty pride and vanity, if Love is not a part of all, the greatest man is very small."

"Two ears and only one mouth have you, the reason I think is clear. It teaches, my child, that it will not do, to talk about all that you hear."

"I just can't write a letter! Every time I begin, I can't find the paper, or I can't find a pen. There are a thousand reasons that you don't hear from me, and at least four of them are sitting here pestering me." Patty

"So be young a little longer, Jan. Let your teenage years keep. Dabble your feet in the brook of life, before you wade in deep. And when you get to be a Mom, and you don't know what to do, remember that your teenage girl, is just a little you." Orene

"You were a lighthouse that stood on a steady shore, guiding us through the rough seas. You were dignity, you were honesty, you were culture, with your understanding and wisdom. You gave us poetry, knowledge and beauty; the ability to see the best in people and in things. And most of all you gave us Love. These things I call the 'Ruth' in me." Carolyn

Aunt Hetty closed by reading me the birth dates of her sisters, including her own, and my mother's at the end of the list.

Odell Arlie (Peel) Vaughn Hutchins, DOB Saturday, July 19, 1913
Orene Alice (Peel) Connell Goff, DOB Tuesday, September 26, 1916
Hetty Jewell (Peel) Moffett, DOB Friday, October 22, 1920
Emma Lou (Peel) Clarke, DOB December 14, 1923
Bonnie Dale (Peel) Connell, DOB Wednesday, March 9, 1927
Patty Evelyn (Peel) Johnston Pearson, DOB September 17, 1930
Robbie Carolyn (Peel) Hall Lampley, DOB May 14, 1936

As she closed the green binder, she brushed away a tear, and a wonderful smile settled back onto her face. I returned the binder to the book shelve as she followed me to the door in her wheelchair. I leaned down and hugged her neck, bidding her farewell, not knowing if I would see her again.

Our visit lingered in my mind for several minutes, as I replayed the beauty of the life that I so admired. Growing old provided us the choice of becoming better or settling for the worse. At some point (and I was drawing closer to that point), I would no longer care what people thought of me, and all the faking that went along with that could end. My visit with Aunt Hetty demonstrated that graceful aging was one of the great freedoms of our human experience. She was free not to recognize other people's expectations and to ignore their opinions. It was right there for the taking. This life was my life, and I regretted how many times I had allowed it to be guided in the wrong direction by outside influence. How was it that so many of life's most important lessons were wasted upon our youth?

Hours passed and my mind emptied of all thought as my hands managed the wheel along AR14. I played songs by *Bruce Hornsby and The Range* the entire trip up the river from Blanchard Springs Caverns to Yellville and along the long climb into the land of the Buffalo. The winding highway kept me wonderfully bathed in forests and pasture along the length of the high balds. People that I saw and waved to along the way seemed to being doing just fine. I passed a stand of beekeeper boxes sitting off the road near Dillard's Ferry, where I stopped in at Wild Bill's Outfitters for gas and a snack. The highway continued from there across the high vistas of the foothills of the Ozarks, still hugging the ridgeline until it split off to the north at AR125 to Buck Creek and onto Peel. The sparse landscape provided periodic long vistas of the rolling plateau with its rolling pastures of thin grass and sage that separated scattered ranch houses and pole barns at every half mile or so. Entering into the Peel community, I was greeted by an old pontoon boat alongside the road, now abandoned to sail only the yard it sat in, still upright and ready for service, as if a great hand had come and deposited it in its spot. It had a small tree growing through the front deck that would require removal in order to make her lake-worthy again. Just up the road from the beached pontoon, the fall hay was rolled into silvery-green bales and sat across a wide, rolling cut field like giant gumdrops. The only traffic I passed was a farmer carrying a round bale on the front of his tractor. A neighbor drove an old Chevy pickup in front of him, providing escort service while never missing a draw on the cigarette that was molded between the fingers of his left hand which rested comfortably on the driver's side cracked mirror. There was certainly plenty of work to be done in these hills, but nobody seemed in too much of a hurry.

The sun hung low in a yellow haze as I made my way down the short road leading to the loading point for Peel Ferry. A small group of motorcyclists wearing black leather and aged faces greeted me at the ramp. The drive from Batesville to Yellville on Highway 14 was uneventful, but inspiring. For most of the trip I followed two couples on Harleys, our sightseeing entourage happy to coast along inside of the speed limit, more interested in taking in the view than getting anywhere quickly, which was fine with me. They deserted me at Buffalo Point, stopping for a view, as I pressed on. I calculated that I would easily reach Peel Ferry well before sunset and did not expect to find it necessary to rush through the day. As it worked out, if this was not the last run from south to north, I would be surprised. I sat in my truck and waited for the ferry to return from the far side, taking in the view of the crystal blue lake and the sandy plateau where it gathered into the wide spot on Bull Shoals. Flashes of yellow sunlight pirouetted across the tops of the ripples on the lake to the west, the dark and light blue patches of water below them exchanging places in an enticing dance with the evening breeze. A quick rush of cool mountain air hit my face. I noticed a small orange floating box and attached barge ambling along the lake's surface in our direction. The water level looked low, the shoreline exposing ten to twelve feet of tumbled stones between the water and the vegetation, and I was unsure if the lake was suffering from a drought or if the authorities had already pulled it down to winter pool.

Within a minute or two, the ferry skidded into place and quickly unloaded the single car coming from the Missouri side. The ride across the water from shore to shore took about fifteen minutes, while my gaze alternated between the aqua-blue water and splendid mountain vistas. The tallest of the trees were still holding onto the last vestige of their fall coloring before the inevitable onslaught of winter days ahead. The ferry's high-strung engine put out an annoying buzzing sound, seemingly straining against the water that flapped against the flat sides of the barge. The cool wind that I had felt earlier now blew steadily from the direction of the sun, gently rocking the ferry from one side to the other in response to its frequent gusts. I stood at the side railing and breathed in as much of the cool air as my lungs would hold. I was alive. I was home.

The heavy steel loading plate of the ferryboat scraped across the worn concrete of the north ramp, startling me out of my thoughts. The ride across Bull Shoals on the ferry had been quicker than I wanted it to be. I returned to my truck, carefully driving off of the ferry back onto Missouri soil, heading east to Danny's lake house just a few miles beyond the Missouri line. I arrived after dusk, where I found Danny standing over a smoking grill tending to what turned out to be the best burgers I have ever eaten.

After supper, Danny stoked some fresh logs into the fire. We grabbed our guitars and played until our fretting fingers gave out and called it a day. The next morning, we were up early, but the weather had other ideas. Despite the gloomy forecast, we hitched Danny's Nitro to the truck and headed for the ramp at the bottom of the hill. Danny and I fished hard all day Sunday, curled up in a ball inside our zippered jackets, working our jigs and grubs relentlessly among the jagged rocks that lined the cold, deep lake. The blast of cool air that I first felt crossing Peel Ferry the day before had now settled into the area as a genuine cold front, carrying with it an ice cold, steady rain. We fought the bad weather for most of the day like troopers, but agreed that if it were raining Monday morning, we would cut short the fishing trip. Even for diehards, it was just too damned cold. At one point on Sunday, my hands were so stiff that I couldn't thread my line through a fishhook eye. We struggled to catch enough to feed ourselves with a decent supper, but by keeping every Crappie we caught, we did manage to catch a mess. The battered fillets joined ample fries and hushpuppies late that evening, and along with a hot fire in the chimney, and a splash or two or more of Jack Daniels, combined to provide excellent sustenance to our bodies and mind. By this time in our fishing lives, one thing we knew how to do well was to cook food favorable to cornmeal and oil. When I needed it the most, laughing my butt off, sipping JD Single Barrel, and playing guitars late into the night, was just what I received, and did so with the good grace and cheerfulness of my valued friend and fellow sojourner. Going fishing with Danny was just an excuse to spend time together. Actually catching fish was our secondary objective. As this trip had conspicuously reminded me, the joy of friendship was in the journey.

Early the next morning, I could hear the rain pounding the tin roof of the lake house. I rose, showered, slipped on some clothes and loaded up my truck. I gave a quick man hug to my old Professor buddy, thanked him liberally for the invitation, and waved goodbye as I pulled out of the gravel driveway, heading south toward Little Rock. The rain looked like it was settling in for the third day in a row. I called Pam to let her know my change in schedule, as I had decided that since I was so close, I would visit my father. She asked me to head home after Little Rock and I said I would, her voice tearing at my insides in all of its tenderness. Sometimes it took separation to clarify in our minds what was really important. I was given this chance to sort out most of it along the way, by looking back, looking ahead, looking to others, and looking at myself. It wasn't that I was afraid to be alone. I was simply more complete when with her. There were no words for what she meant to me.

Chapter 15

« CRYSTAL HILL »

With Missouri behind me, I followed the Ozark Plateau south along the highland rim through Bear Creek Springs, Harrison, and Western Grove. The contour of the main north-south highway mirrored the path of rainwater runoff from these high barrens, which seeped through the sandstone, filling the Buffalo River in preparation of its plunge into the gorge of the Salem Plateau at the feet of Push Mountain. Within every few miles after crossing the Buffalo River, there were sights and places that brought back memories and emotions of earlier times that I wished had been more appreciated. Memories were a tricky thing in our human experience. Over time, they tended to grow in favor or diminish in importance, based upon the filter we ran them through. The people, times, and places that we looked back upon with only fond recollection may not have been that pleasant in the reality of the experience. Likewise, judgments of condemnation that we rendered in light of the perspective of time, far removed from the context, perhaps deserved reconsideration. Context is a vital, irreplaceable component of judgment, and without it, our memories morph into what we believed them to be as much as what they actually were. Truth was never an easy sort.

For years, I kept a picture of my father and me walking along the pebble-ridden banks of Mill Creek, where it dumped into the Buffalo at Tyler Bend. I could not have been more than seven or eight years old at the time. As I walked down the narrow pathway from the Visitor's Center, I tried to remember that day with my family and walking along the bank with my Dad, my short arms reaching up to hold his hand. I remember a picnic spread across one of the park's tables, and my sisters splashing water on each other in the shallow portions of the river. I stepped out onto the creek gravel shoal that framed the great bend in the unimpeded natural river. The bluffs hovered above me in a grand canopy of colored leaves. People were milling about the area, dipping their toes into the water to check its temperature. I thought about the forty-five years since I had stood right here with my Dad holding me on his shoulders with his large hands. I recalled how his hands felt and looked as he held me firm. They were dry and rough, like the hands of a man that worked them for his living. His knuckles were knobby and twisted from his early years as a catcher playing semi-pro baseball. He had a strong grip and a firm handshake. When my sisters and I were small children, my father would sometimes take us and toss us into the air, floating free for just a few seconds, only to return to his safe, strong grip. This was such a joy for us kids, and I remember pestering my tiring father to repeat the toss until he was forced completely out of energy. The joy was in the freedom of flying, but only so when knowing that we would be gathered in the fall. My earthly father was no longer here to toss me into the air, and I was no longer a child to receive it, but there was a greater blessing for me, of tossing my own children and a grandchild into the air. Time passes the baton. As I loved and lived inside of the regrets of my own imperfections, the trees above my head, the stones below my feet, and the water within my sight painted the memories that spoke to the love that I held for my father inside of his imperfections. I needed the same grace from my children that my Dad deserved from me. Honor for his long sacrifice and forgiveness for his failings was all any father hoped for. This was the thread that bound the generations together, where continuing to love was always the choice over contrary reasons, and compassion required no payment.

I wanted to reach his gravesite while I still had light, and the evening was noticeably beginning to shorten. The main reason I left Arkansas the last time was the same reason that had kept me from coming back, but passing by miles of memories, where the good had mostly crowded out the bad, made me feel a part of its dirt again. From Conway to Little Rock, I thought about my parents' volatile relationship with one another, and how we children hid beneath our beds during some of their more heated arguments. They fought a lot, and I remembered Mom gathering us together one day when we lived in Brownsville, solemnly asking us if we wanted to go live with our father or stay with her. We had to make the choice. I was in the 4th grade, Tina in the 3rd grade, and Robin a year away from kindergarten. We could barely comprehend what she was even saying, much less weigh the profound gravity of the circumstances. Obviously, this was a mechanism for our mother to reach our father, demonstrating to him the torment that would result in his children should they divorce. Not unlike so many women of that time, my mother was wholly unprepared to face life without my father. She had long since abandoned whatever educational or professional objectives she harbored as a young woman, and there in Brownsville, faced with a marriage that was about to break apart, her fear of being alone was so emotionally overwhelming that she was willing to leverage tremendous emotional stress onto her small children as a means of protecting herself. My Dad knew fully well that my mom was incapable of taking care of us outside of his participation, and so somehow, they patched it up, and move onto another city, always hoping for something better up ahead.

She was the same woman, twenty years removed from Brownsville, who lived alone in El Dorado for months, struggling to wind down the business while my father took a buyer's job in Memphis just to pay the bills. The same woman always told my sisters and me that we could be whatever we could dream and pushed us to excel academically. The same woman introduced us to the arts and demonstrated her creativity through her painting. The same woman stood at my father's bedside for three weeks, praying for his recovery from heart surgery and against an ensuing staph infection that forced the removal of a section of his breastbone. We buried him a few days later next to his parents in

Little Rock. I could not imagine the horror that was my mother's during that time. She leaned on my father for so much and for so long that she had to be terrified at facing life without him. In many ways, she was just then, in her mid-forties, facing the full weight of life. The times and places they lived in, distilled by a 1950s southern white, evangelical culture, wrapped boundaries around my mother's potential and possibilities that would not be tolerated by my daughters. Mother was as much a victim of her time as she was an accomplice to it. A dichotomy of human frailty and courage never existed more pronounced than it did in my mother, who was a person impossible to adore, far too emotionally distant for consolation, but so often too courageous not to admire. She faced the world she was left alone in with grit - if little else. I long now even as an old man for a reconciliation with her of full understanding, which I realize will never come. We have both long since stopped trying to understand one another. Only my father seemed to unveil the best of my mother, even in times of what looked to most like constant chaos. That was the stuff of their true love, and that was as it was with them.

The last time I saw my father before his fatal heart attack was at the Fairview exit off of Interstate 40 on the edge of Dickson County. It was a stormy evening and he had called me to let me know that he would be dropping by on his way back home to Memphis. I sat in his car where we chatted for only a few minutes about how we were both doing. All he talked about was my mother, and how much he regretted having to leave her for so long in El Dorado. My father's legal troubles remained, and he had recently been diagnosed with severe heart disease. After about ten minutes, Dad looked at me and said, *"Son, I've got to get on the road. Your Mom is waiting on me."* I looked at him that night for the first time and saw an old man looking back at me, tired and worn out by life. As he pulled away, I knew that whatever chasms had been created over the years between my mother and him had been bridged many times over by forgiveness and mutual dependency. A few months later, I buried my Dad in the full knowledge that despite all of their individual frailties, they were as firmly bound to one another as God could ordain. I know that a large portion of their bond was sealed through mutual suffering, as scars heal stronger than untouched skin. The remaining part was sealed in steadfastness to each other through it all. I wanted that to be the story of Pam and Kenny. The best part of what my parents had for one another was what I wanted for us. We would wear our scars for the world to see. We would wear them while holding on to one another.

It was mid-afternoon by the time I reached Roselawn Cemetery off of Asher Avenue, where my father's grave lay beneath the shade of a Holly tree. I rarely visited here, except for that one time when I had left Tennessee at midnight to drive seven hours directly to Dad's grave, flowers and a card in hand. I am yet to understand what longing compelled me to come so far, but it was as if my father was calling to me across the miles. I left the flowers and the card on Dad's grave. I wrote on the card, *"Dad. I miss you greatly and love you more than I ever told you."* As I walked away from his grave, glancing back for a last look, I remembered how deeply he adored my mother, and how hard that love had been earned. The strongest iron was forged from life's hottest fire and with its richest ore, found scarcely scattered among the dirt of our beginnings. Maybe I knew why I came there after all. The dirt gave us its best and gathered its best back to it.

As I readied to leave, rays of sunshine caught my eye as they sifted through the beautiful Holly tree that stood beside my father's grave. The clouds had broken. I reached up and grabbed a low limb, and pinched a pointed leaf from the tree. God worked, not in the realm of astonishment, but in the realm of forbearance. He was not a God with a bag of magic tricks. His miracles were built into the design, and people were His masterpiece. To find Him, I had to be willing to trust the mystery of time and circumstance, and embrace the obscurity of unconditional love and forgiveness. All of these things were impossible for me to do, outside of suffering, which opened me up to see what God was really about. The healing would only be found coming out of the pain. Again, maybe I knew why I came.

Evening sat in as I drove downtown from Roselawn Cemetery and checked into a room at the downtown Marriott overlooking the river along West Markham Street. This main artery that followed the river upstream dead-ended into old Union Station, a place where I spent hours and hours as a child roaming around the depot and the train yard. My grandmother would give me a quarter so that I could buy a Coke at the gift shop inside. After checking in, I drove down Markham and circled through the Union Station entrance area. Despite its obvious renovation, the once active train depot looked much like it did forty years ago when I was free to run across the wide yard without impediment. The same level of security was enforced at the State Capitol Building just up the street from Union Station, where I would walk the halls among the legislative staff and even ventured into an elevator a time or two. Unbeknownst to me at the time, a freak accident in one of those elevators inside the state building caused the untimely death of an Arkansas State Representative, Ira Marvin Gurley, in the year 1932. Representative Gurley was a resident of Green Forest, Arkansas, in the northwestern part of the state. He was also the father of Helen Gurley Brown, the famous feminist author and magazine editor, who decried her Arkansas upbringing as "raised among hicks" and rarely wished to discuss it. I am sure if my father had been killed by a state-owned elevator I would hold the state in similar contempt.

Restless and returning to the hotel, I parked and then walked out of the hotel front entrance and circled around a side alleyway, crossing La Harpe Boulevard into Riverfront Park and took a seat on the grass tier overlooking the Arkansas River. The stars were out, but the night sky was still young and the lights of the city hid most of them from my view. The river drifted slowly downstream toward the east, as the current created swirling motions around the large pylons that held up the bridge. I knew where the water was headed, because I had been there. I could see it in my mind's eye, as the currents floated by the high embankment of Arkansas Post that would gather at the #2 Pool Lock north of Dumas and narrow into one channel. Soon it would cross a dozen sand bars and oxbow turn-backs as it merged with the magnificent Mississippi River near Arkansas City. In about six hours, all that water would be pouring into the Gulf of Mexico.

I sat for several minutes in the grass along the riverbank, listening to the dampened and distant sounds of the city and watching the river move with powerful ease. The sky darkened to the point that I could just pick out the bright planet Venus along the elliptical. My eyes panned for the smaller, ruddy Mars, and I found her, blinking a hint of her red surface through thousands of miles of light. I knew that across the vast blackness of space, in a silence too pure to imagine, the two moons of Mars moved along their orbits, without testimony, guided only by the hand of God. One moon was named Fear and the other Dread. For reasons I did not understand – they haunted my dreams.

My cell phone rang and it was my youngest daughter, Mandy, who was finishing up her senior year of nursing school at Austin Peay State University in Clarksville, Tennessee. She apologized for calling me so late on a weeknight, and I shared with her that I was out of town on a fishing trip. The reason for her call was to tell me how she had taken the old highway back through northern Alabama on her way to Tennessee the previous day and had stopped at a small store for gas. While there, she noticed a display of local honey for sale. Knowing how much I loved locally produced honey, she bought me a jar and told me she would bring it to me on her next visit home. She said, *"It's from Bill's Honey Farm. Meridianville, Alabama."*

Her thoughtfulness made me smile. I thanked her and asked, *"Where was it that you stopped and bought the honey? Do you remember the name of the town?"*

"I think it was called Paint Rock," she replied. *"It was basically in the middle of nowhere. I'm pretty sure it was Paint Rock, Alabama."*

After thanking Mandy again and telling her I loved her, I hung up. Was there anything a father cherished more than a call from his children? I thought not. A grin formed across my face as I marveled in the wonder of how we continued to circle around inside of the same wonderful world that others had circled around inside of before us. From generation to generation, the same orbits bounded out paths. Paint Rock, Alabama was where my 4th-great-grandfather on the Hall side, James Carter Hall, settled and died. He moved first to Kentucky from North Carolina in the late 1700s, and then passed away in Jackson County, Alabama, in 1870, after serving alongside Davy Crockett in the War of 1812. It was a family land grant earned from his service which sparked his son, my 3rd-great-grandfather, to migrate west to the Arkansas territory to claim it.

I stood up, brushing away the grass from my dampened backside, and walked back up the alleyway into the hotel. The lobby bar on the first floor was still strangely active, and I could hear loud music playing with many louder voices trying to talk over it. While waiting for the elevator to arrive at the first floor, I recognized the song playing in the bar. It was one of my favorite tunes. I knew the name of the songwriter who had penned its lyrics, a Baptist preacher's kid, and I likewise knew the voice of the artist who sang this version's last stanza. I had driven by his childhood home on many occasions when I worked for my father in El Dorado. The small yellow brick building that housed the neighborhood school was a regular customer of H & H Distributing. I had not the occasion to travel through Kingsland, Arkansas in many years, but the last time I was there, thirty years ago, the school was the largest building in town. Johnny Cash found his way out of that small town and into music history, and into this song, among hundreds of others. Listening to Cash artfully deliver the last verse of the famous Jimmy Webb song, *The Highwayman*, I stepped onto the elevator, thinking about home, and Pam, and yes, of the land of my birth. Perhaps one day I would also be back again to rest my spirit if I can.

"I'll fly a starship, across the universe divide. And when I reach the other side, I'll find a place to rest my spirit if I can. Perhaps I may become a highwayman again. Or, I may simply be a single drop of rain; but I will remain – and I'll be back again – and again – and again – and again – and again – and again – and again." (Jimmy Webb, *The Highwayman*)

THE END

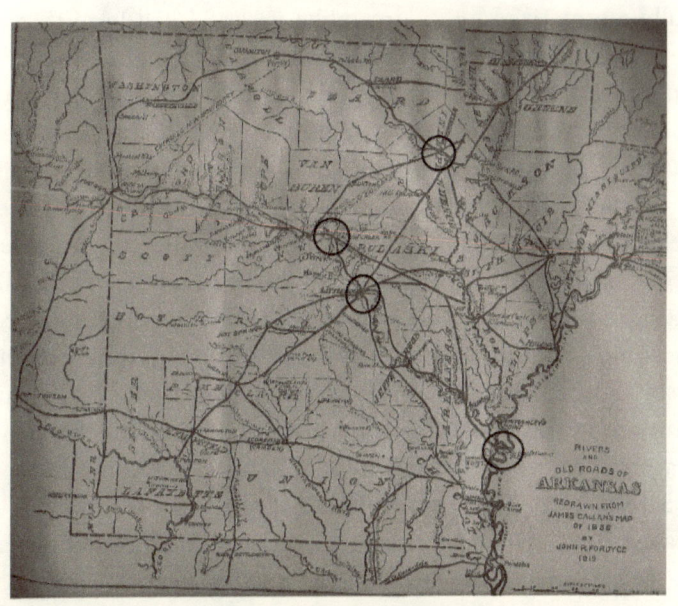

1836 Map of Arkansas

« ACKNOWLEDGMENT »

I first heard about W. G. Sebald and *The Rings of Saturn* when I ran across the documentary of Sebald's Suffolk County wanderings entitled, *Patience (After Sebald)*, written and filmed by Grant Gee and distributed by Cinema Guild. I immediately picked up a copy of the book and read it in a few short days, totally mesmerized by its dreamlike prose. I had been thinking about this manuscript for months and had not quite found the framework that I felt would enable me to pursue the tapestry of geometries and connecting points that were floating around in my head. Sebald's eclectic book, more than any other, inspired the format of *The Two Moons of Mars*, and I am eternally grateful for having stumbled across his masterwork at just the time that I needed inspiration to bring my own thoughts into focus. Sebald's writing is pure genius and anyone who will take the time to read *The Rings of Saturn* will see the world through a different set of lenses and visit places that they never knew existed. As I tried to point out in this effort, there are magical connections happening all around us every day, and most pass us by without notice. W. G. Sebald opened my eyes to these threads of life, and it is my greatest hope, bowing beneath his genius and inspiration, that *The Two Moons of Mars* will do the same for you.

It takes a lot of work to write a book. My friend and editor Brian Darnell stood shoulder to shoulder with me during the years of "*Moons*". The best of what you found inside these pages reflects his immense gifts and talents. Thank you Brian.

Kenneth Hall

The Two Moons of Mars is the first book by author, entrepreneur, and educator, Kenneth Hall. Most recently Hall co-founded and now manages a precious metals research facility near Atlanta. Hall holds a doctoral degree in Organizational Management, reflecting his research and focus on Formal Axiology and the study of human values and organizational ethics. He resides with his wife, Pam, and their three dogs in northern Georgia.

The Two Moons of Mars is published by Doghouse Dreams LLC, http://www.doghousedreams.com